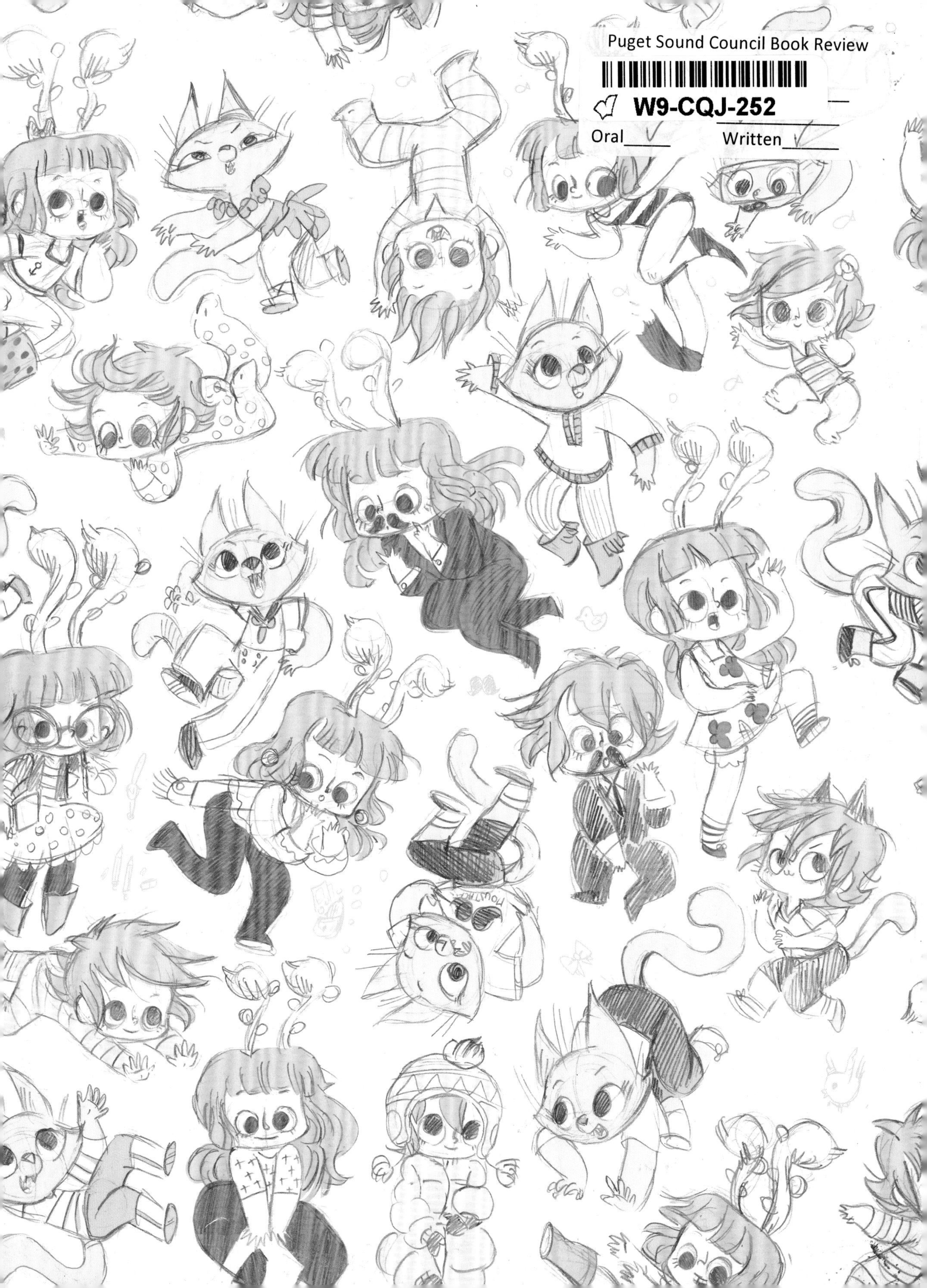

THE WHISKERS SISTERS

#1 MAY'S WILD WALK

MissPATY

GRAPHIC UNIVERSE™ • MINNEAPOLIS

Story and illustrations by MissPATY
Translation by Nathan Sacks

First American edition published in 2017 by Graphic Universe™

Les Soeurs Moustaches, Tome 1: La balade de Maï
Copyright © 2014 by Éditions Sarbacane, Paris.
Published by arrangement with Sylvain Coissard Agency in cooperation with Nicolas Grivel Agency

Graphic Universe™ is a trademark of Lerner Publishing Group, Inc.

Graphic Universe™
A division of Lerner Publishing Group, Inc.
241 First Avenue North
Minneapolis, MN 55401 USA

For reading levels and more information, look up this title at www.lernerbooks.com.

Main body text set in AndyStd-Regular 12/14
Typeface provided by Monotype Typography

Library of Congress Cataloging-in-Publication Data

Names: Miss Paty, 1979- author, illustrator. | Sacks, Nathan, translator.
Title: May's wild walk / story and illustrations by Miss Paty ; translation by Nathan Sacks.
Other titles: Balade de Mai. English
Description: First American edition. | Minneapolis : Graphic Universe, 2017. | Series: The Whisker sisters |
    Summary: Ignored by her sisters while they plan a party, baby May crawls into the letter carrier's bag and is
    transported into the woods, where she meets animals who are ready to play.
Identifiers: LCCN 2016024478 | ISBN 9781512425277 (lb : alk. paper)
Subjects: LCSH: Graphic novels. | CYAC: Graphic novels. | Sisters—Fiction. | Forest animals—Fiction. |
    Babies—Fiction.
Classification: LCC PZ7.7.M515 May 2017 | DDC 741.5/973—dc23

LC record available at https://lccn.loc.gov/2016024478

Manufactured in the United States of America
1-41273-23240-10/21/2016

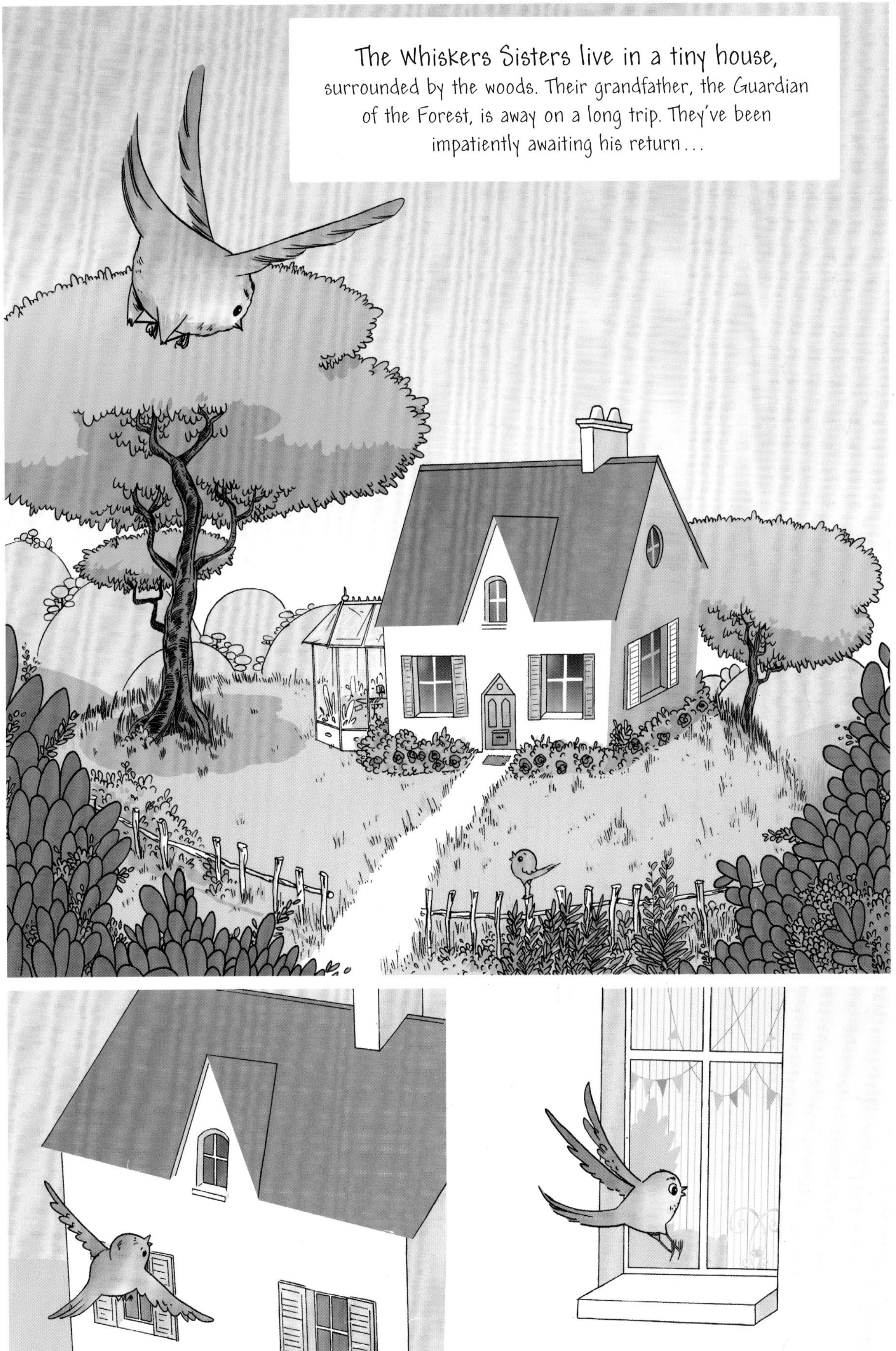
The Whiskers Sisters live in a tiny house, surrounded by the woods. Their grandfather, the Guardian of the Forest, is away on a long trip. They've been impatiently awaiting his return...

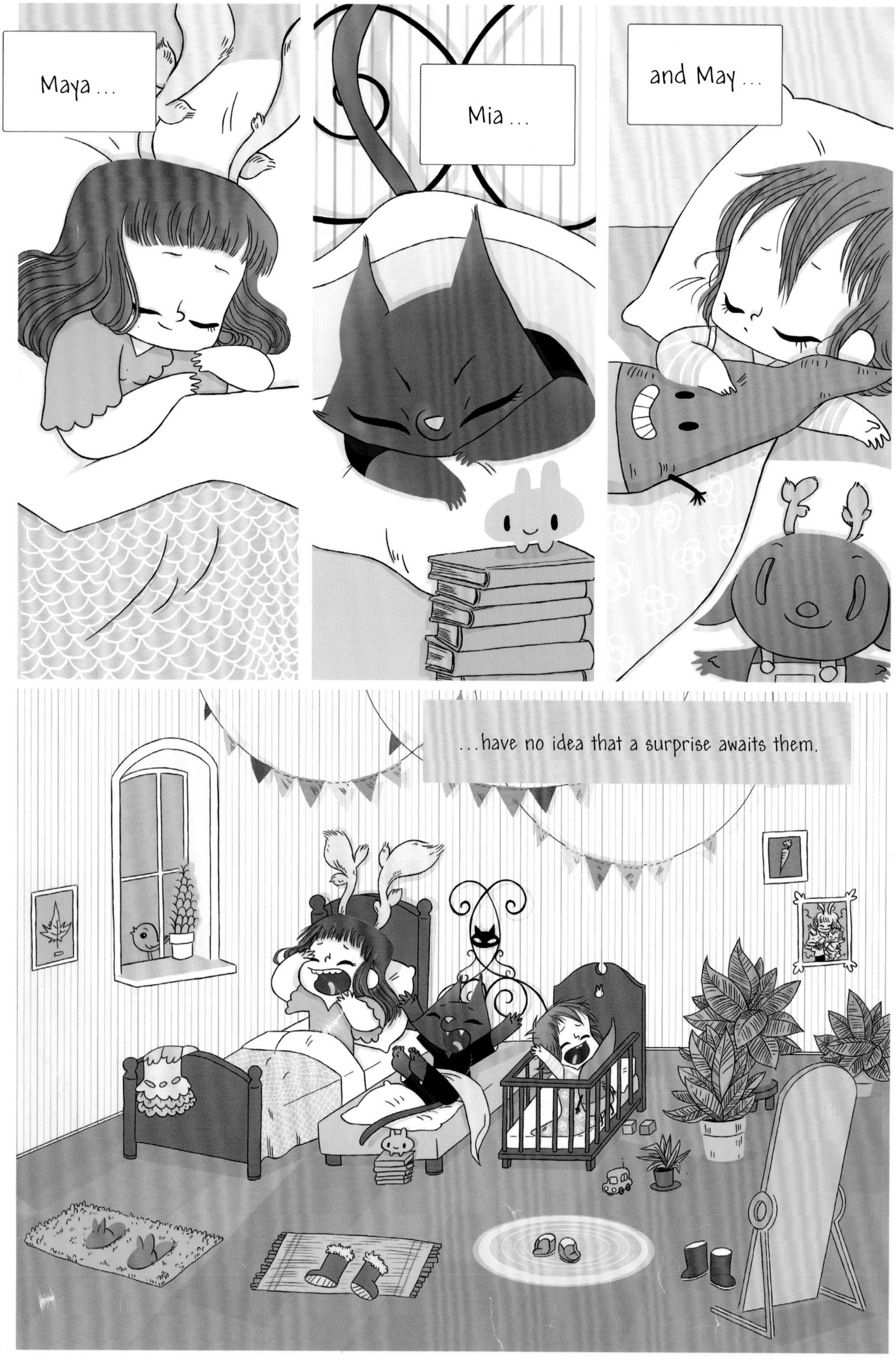
Maya...
Mia...
and May...
...have no idea that a surprise awaits them.

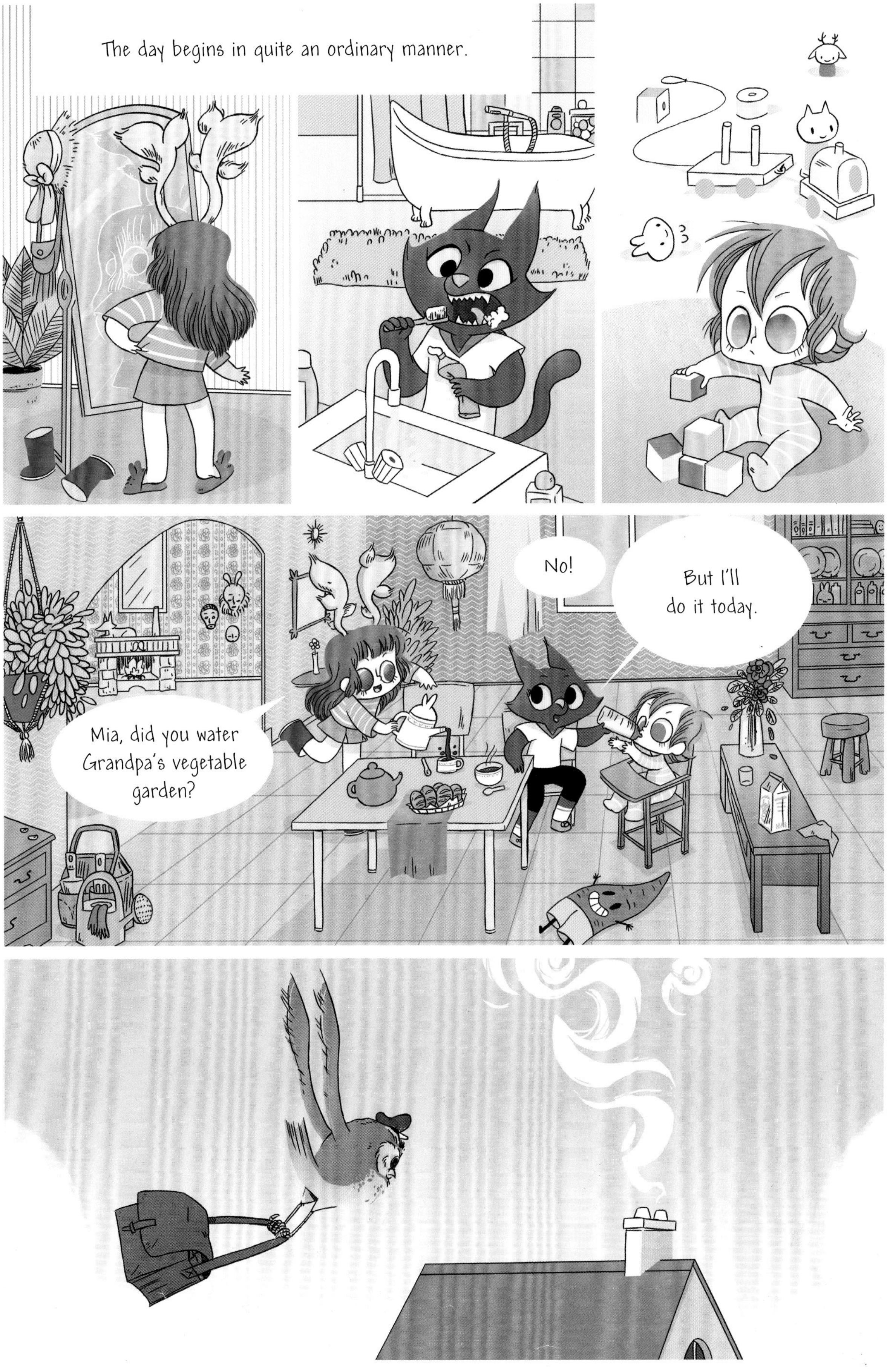
The day begins in quite an ordinary manner.
Mia, did you water Grandpa's vegetable garden?
No!
But I'll do it today.

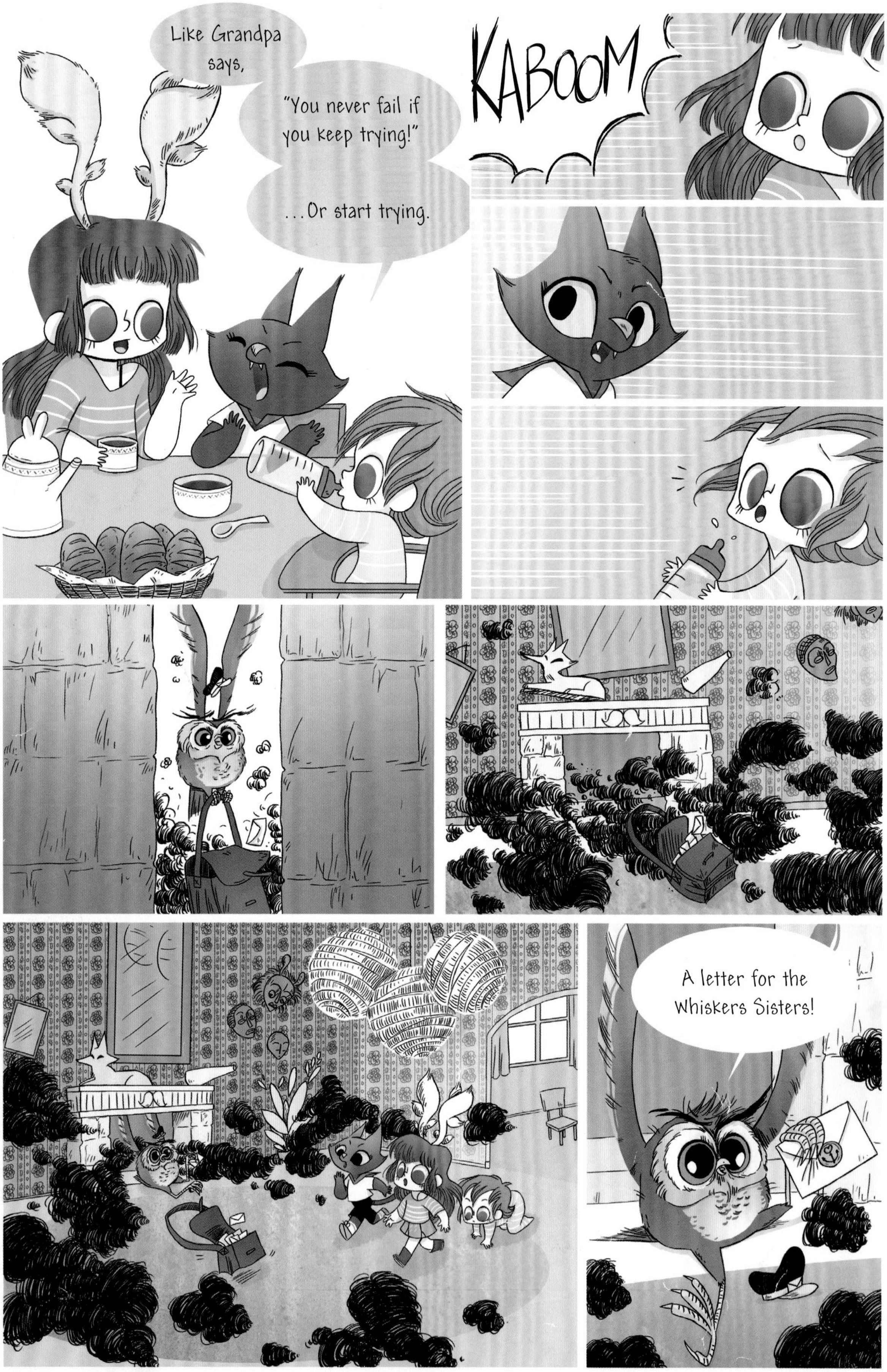
Like Grandpa says,
"You never fail if you keep trying!"
...Or start trying.
KABOOM
A letter for the Whiskers Sisters!

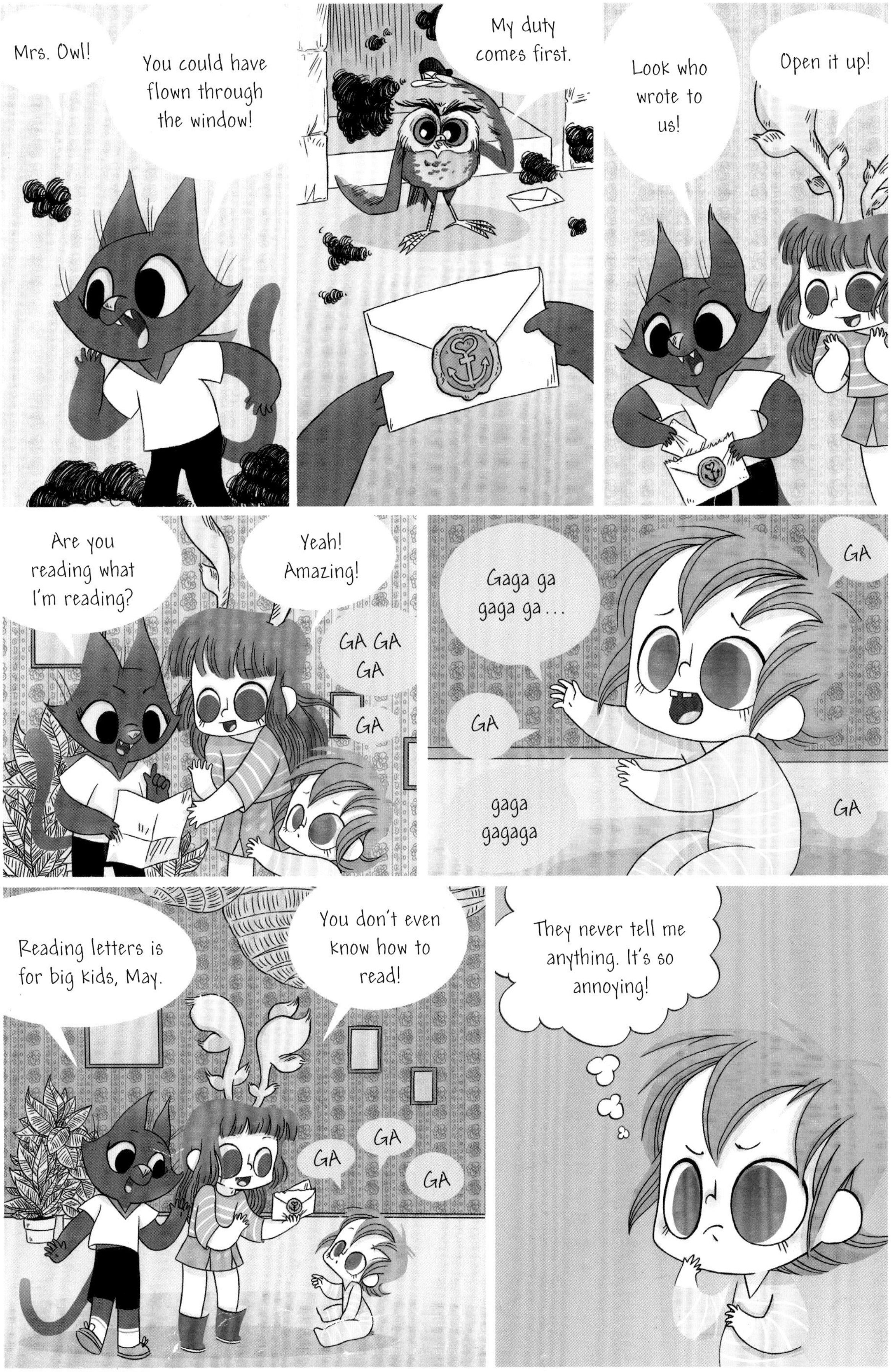
Mrs. Owl!
You could have flown through the window!
My duty comes first.
Look who wrote to us!
Open it up!
Are you reading what I'm reading?
Yeah! Amazing!
GA GA GA
GA
Gaga ga gaga ga...
GA
GA
gaga gagaga
GA
Reading letters is for big kids, May.
You don't even know how to read!
GA
GA
GA
They never tell me anything. It's so annoying!

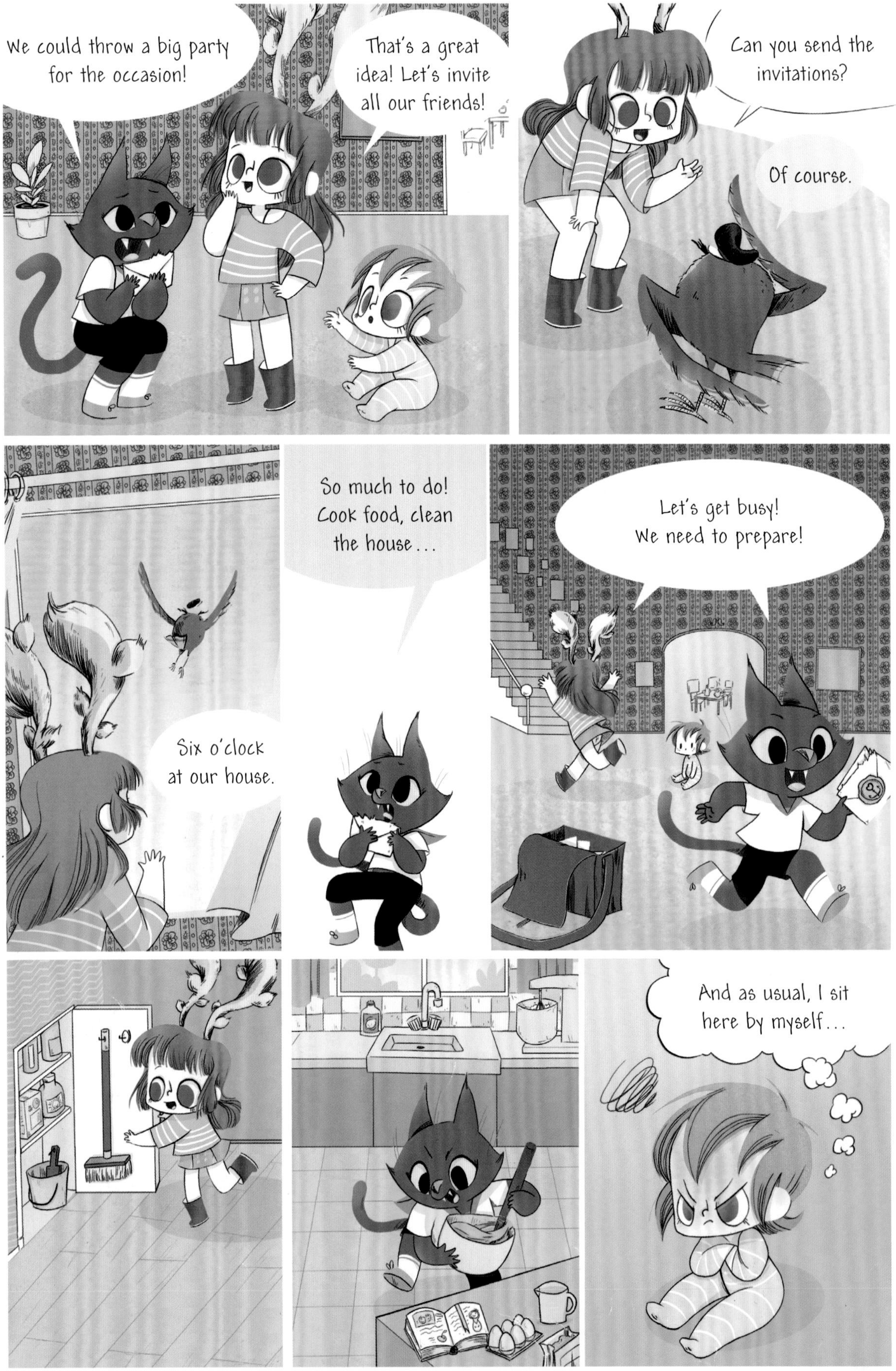
We could throw a big party for the occasion!
That's a great idea! Let's invite all our friends!
Can you send the invitations?
Of course.
Six o'clock at our house.
So much to do! Cook food, clean the house...
Let's get busy! We need to prepare!
And as usual, I sit here by myself...

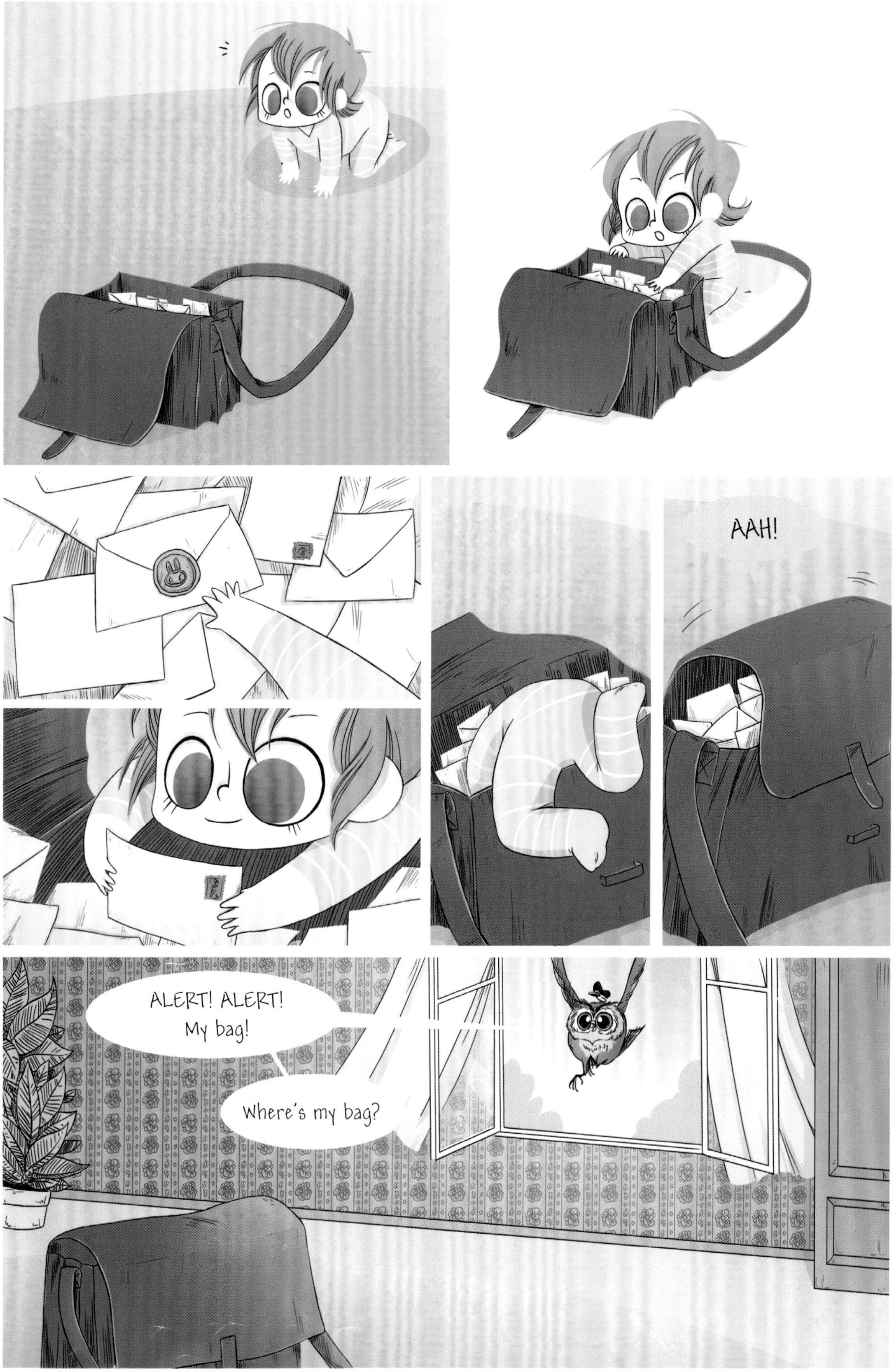
AAH!
ALERT! ALERT!
My bag!
Where's my bag?

Phew!
There it is.

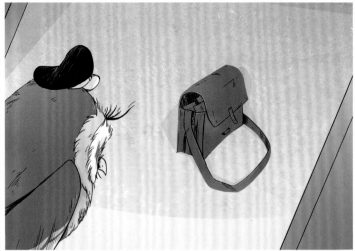

Goodness,
it's heavy!

Mia, have you seen May?

Ah, she's probably out playing somewhere!

Olympic View Library
2626 SW 327th
Federal Way, WA 98023

 11

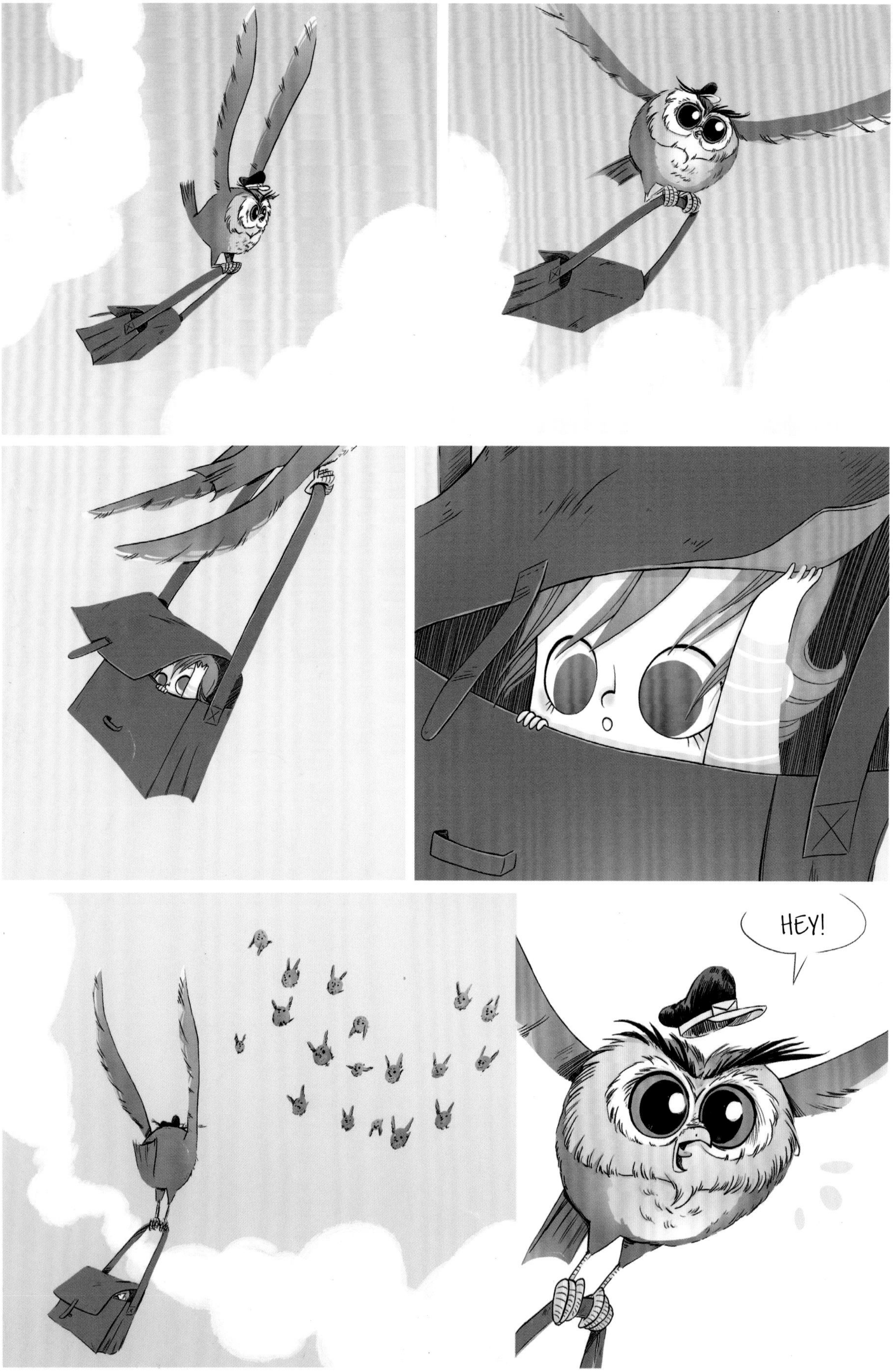
HEY!

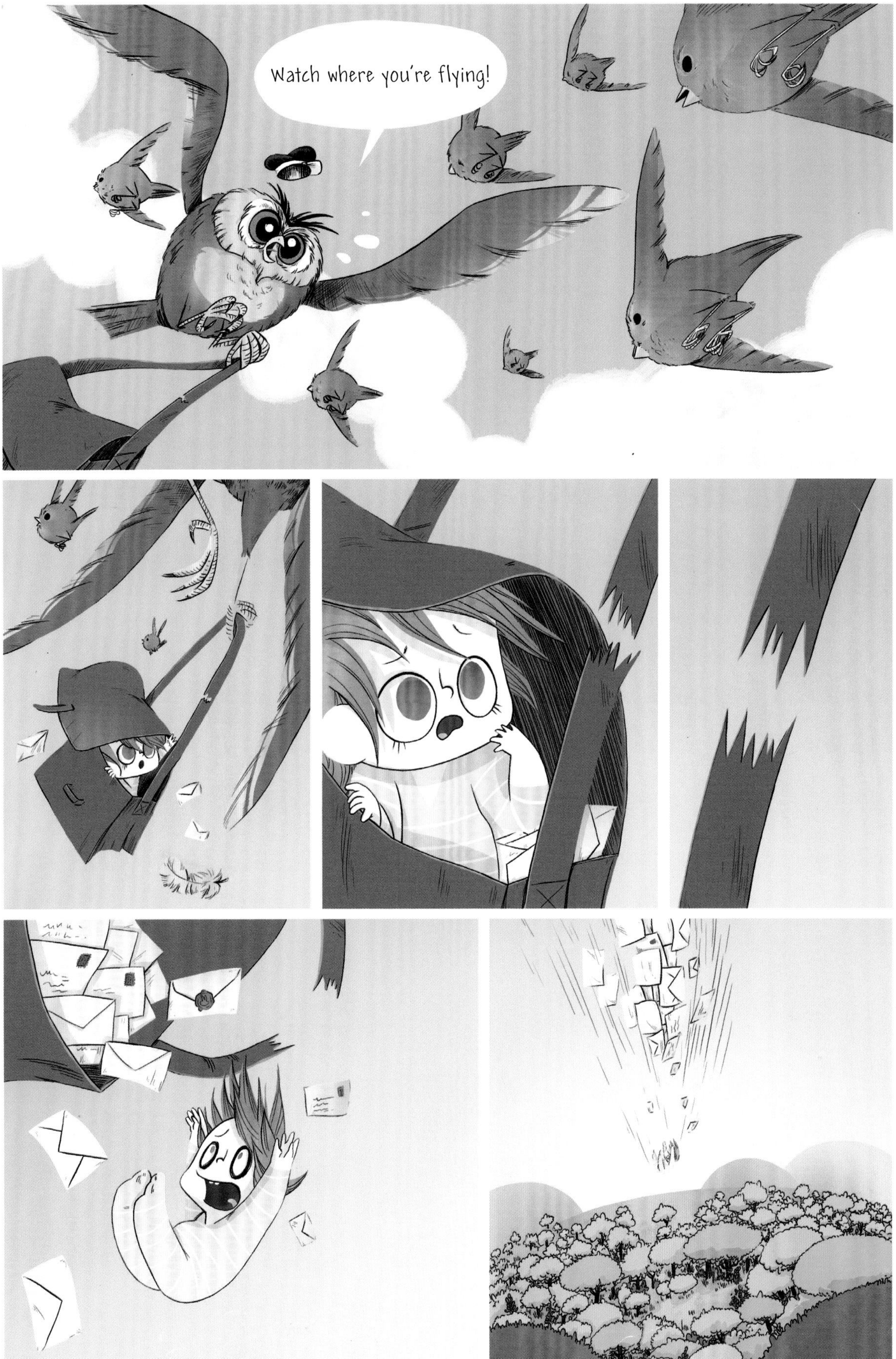
Watch where you're flying!

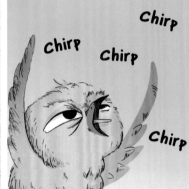

Chirp

Chirp

Chirp

Chirp

Chirp

Chirp

Chirp

Chirp

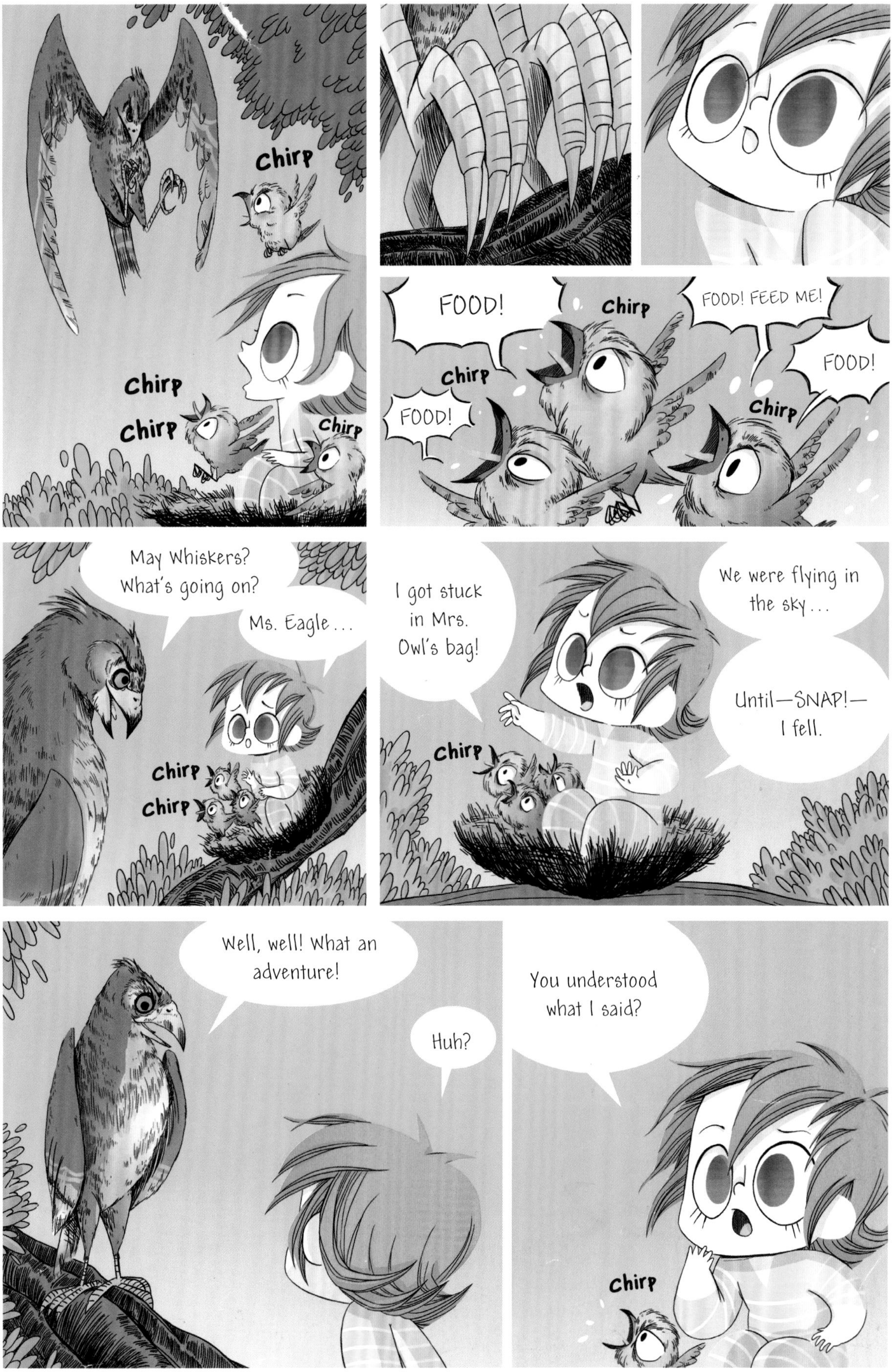
Chirp
Chirp
Chirp
Chirp
FOOD!
Chirp
FOOD! FEED ME!
Chirp
FOOD!
FOOD!
Chirp
May Whiskers?
What's going on?
Ms. Eagle...
Chirp
Chirp
I got stuck in Mrs. Owl's bag!
We were flying in the sky...
Until—SNAP!—I fell.
Chirp
Well, well! What an adventure!
Huh?
You understood what I said?
Chirp

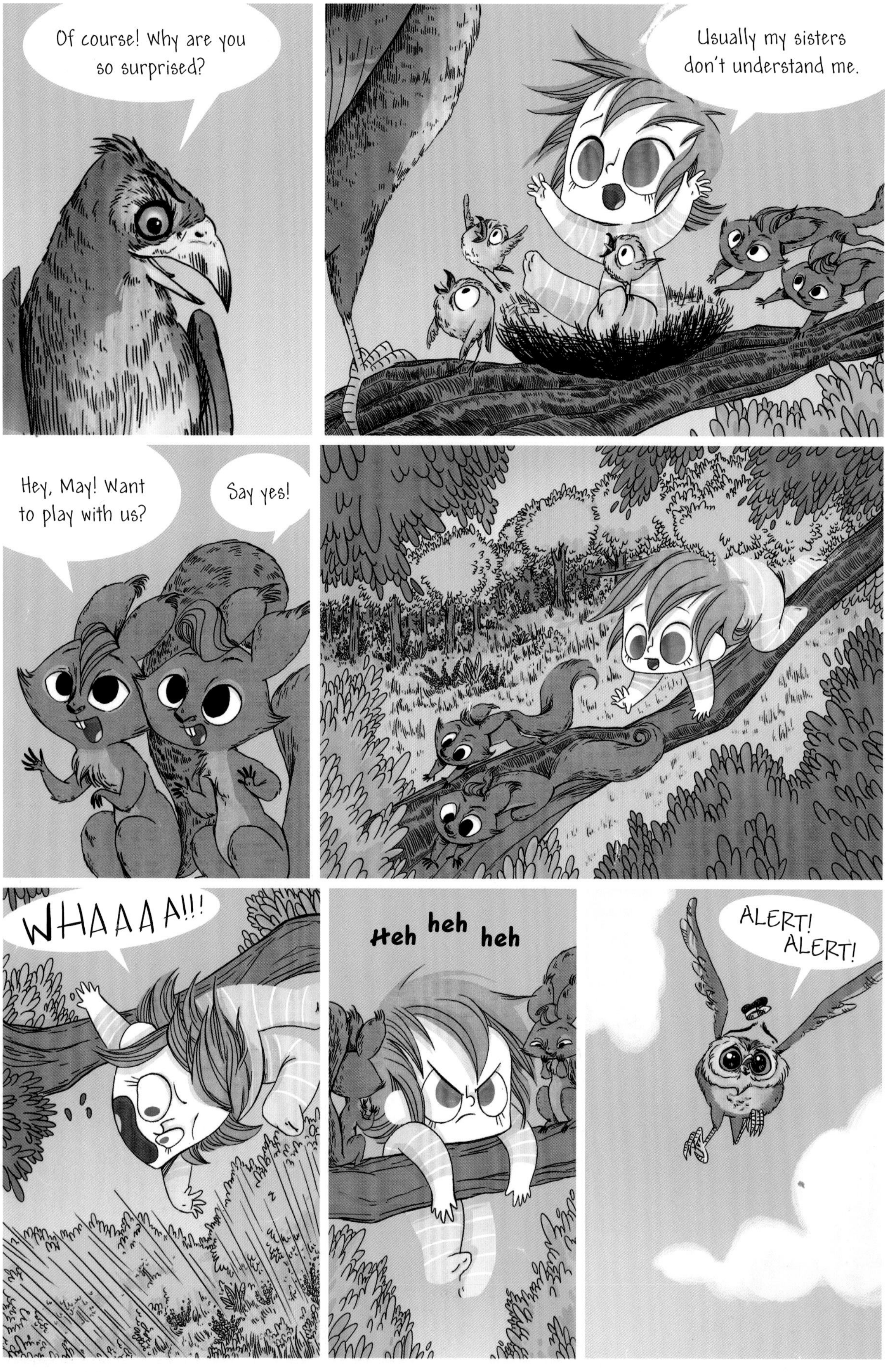

Of course! Why are you so surprised?
Usually my sisters don't understand me.
Hey, May! Want to play with us?
Say yes!
WHAAAA!!!
Heh heh heh
ALERT! ALERT!

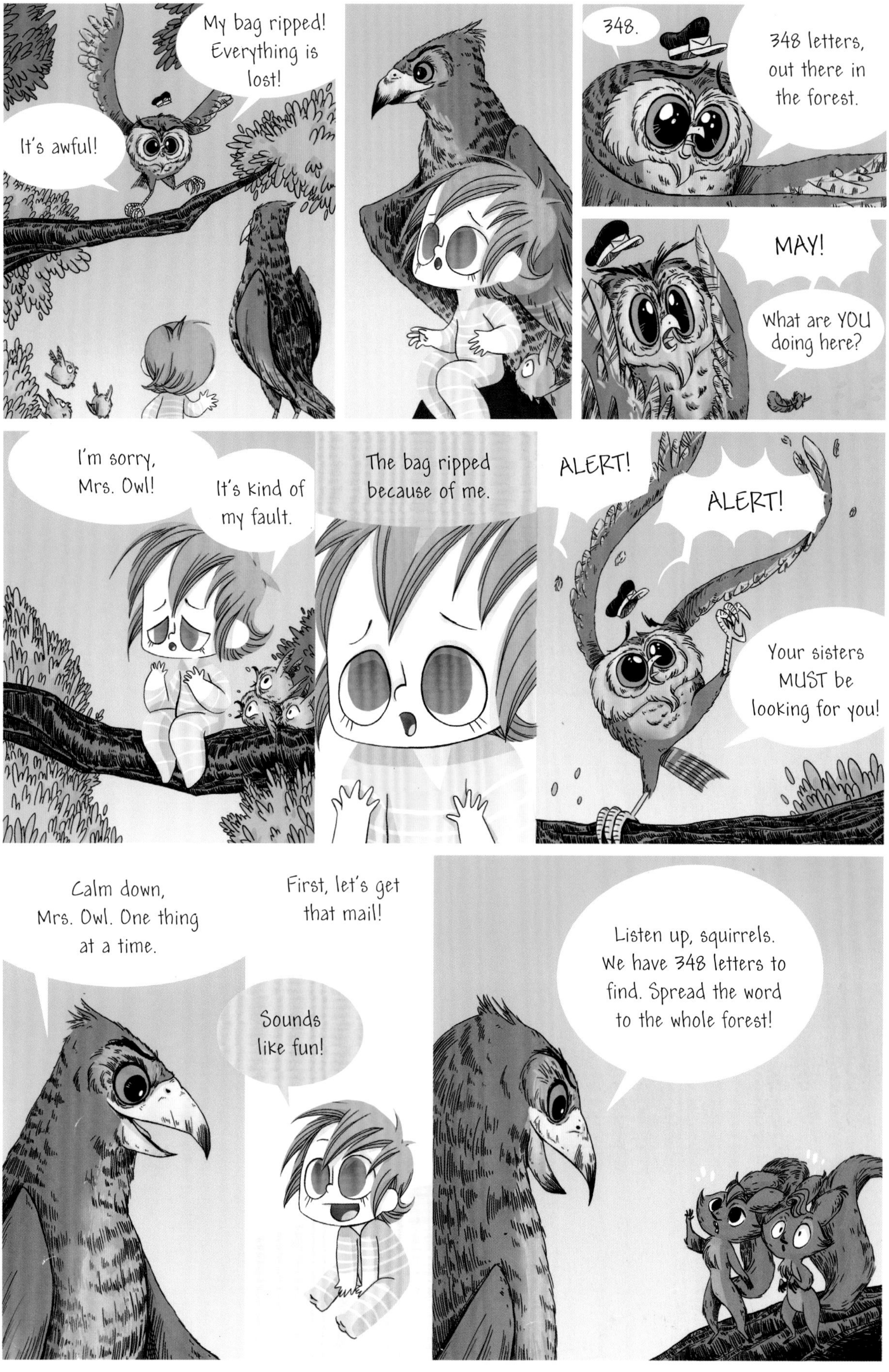
My bag ripped! Everything is lost!
It's awful!
348.
348 letters, out there in the forest.
MAY!
What are YOU doing here?
I'm sorry, Mrs. Owl!
It's kind of my fault.
The bag ripped because of me.
ALERT!
ALERT!
Your sisters MUST be looking for you!
Calm down, Mrs. Owl. One thing at a time.
First, let's get that mail!
Sounds like fun!
Listen up, squirrels. We have 348 letters to find. Spread the word to the whole forest!

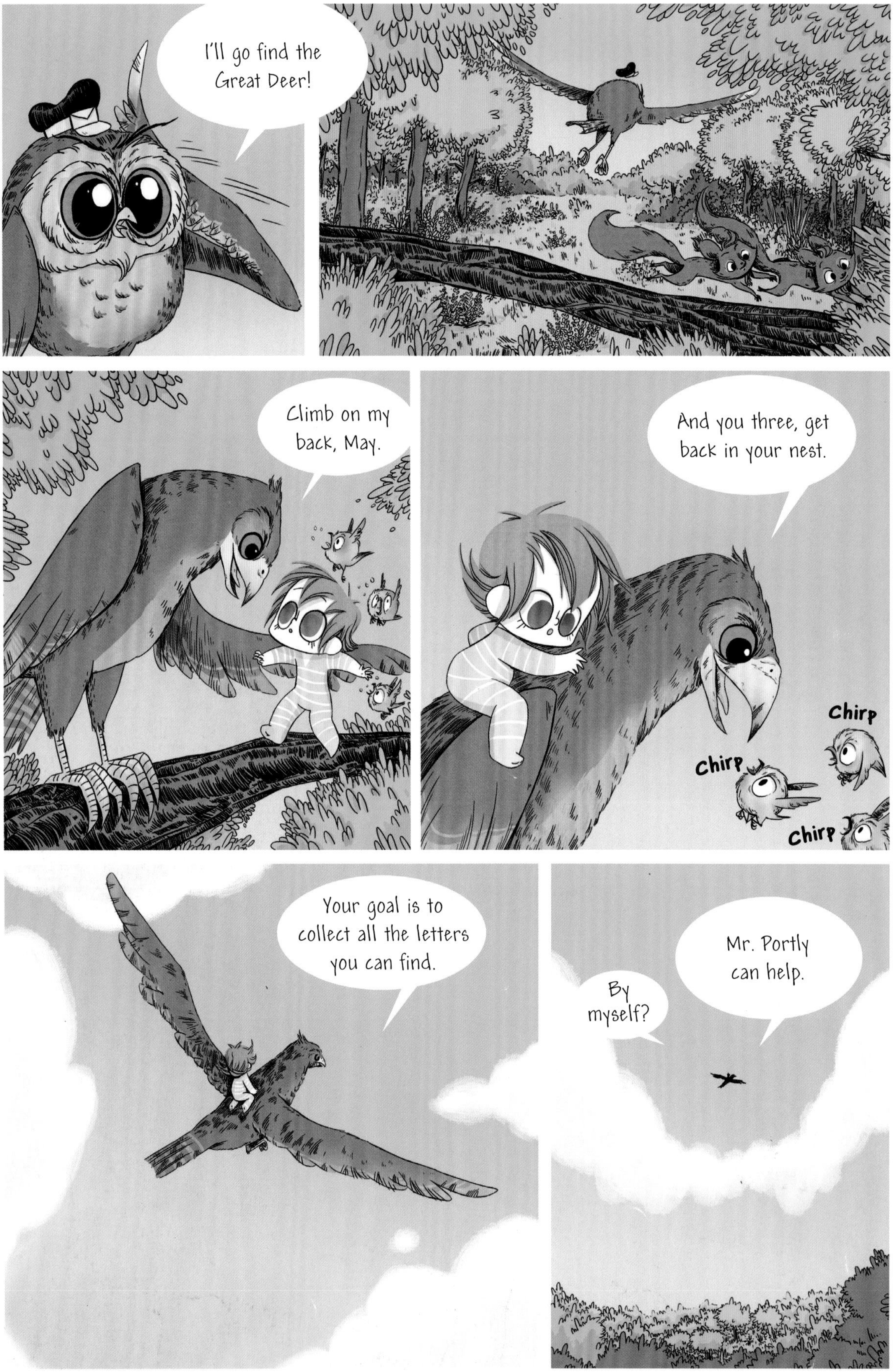
I'll go find the Great Deer!
Climb on my back, May.
And you three, get back in your nest.
Chirp
Chirp
Chirp
Your goal is to collect all the letters you can find.
Mr. Portly can help.
By myself?

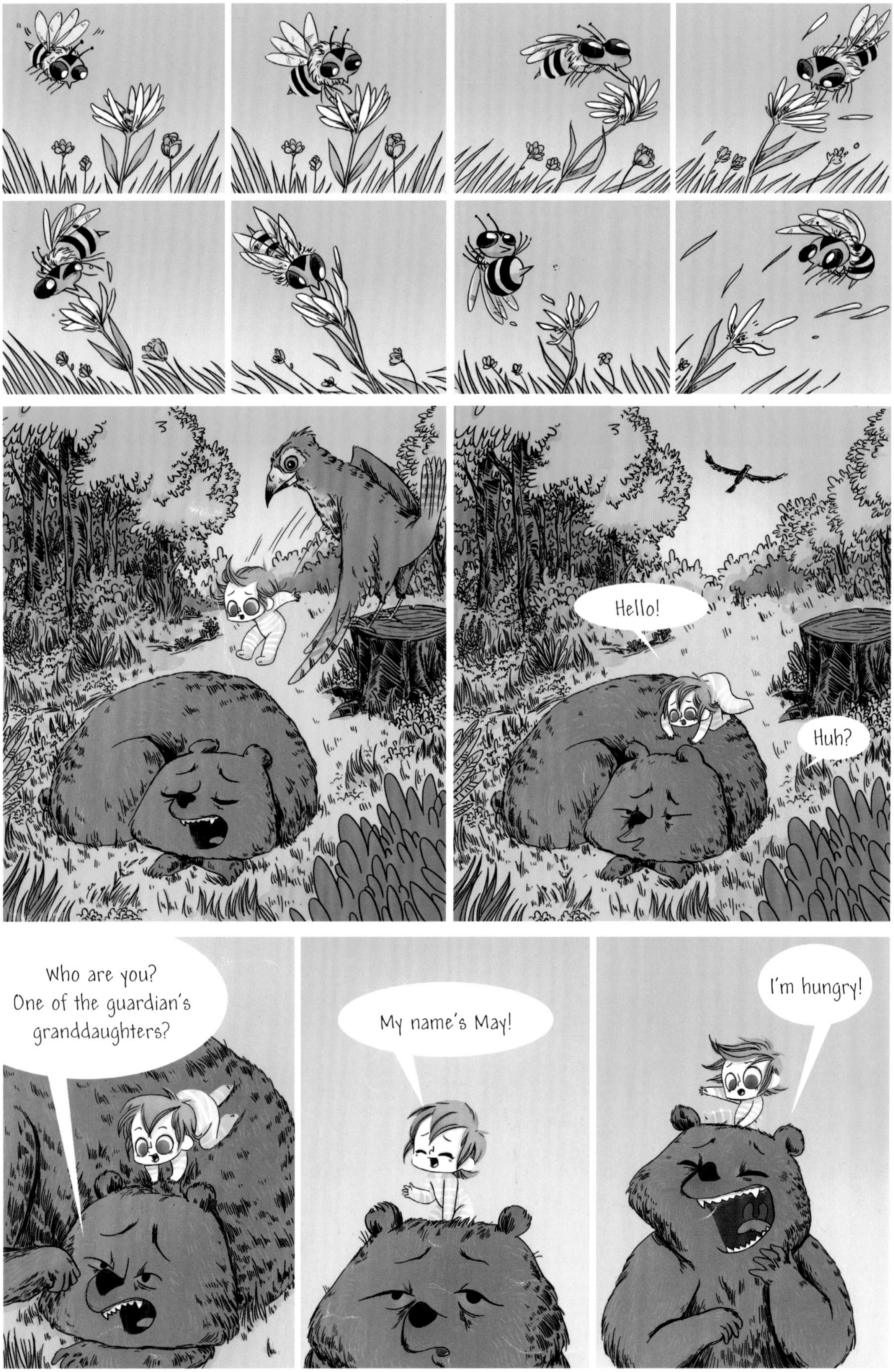
Hello!
Huh?
Who are you? One of the guardian's granddaughters?
My name's May!
I'm hungry!

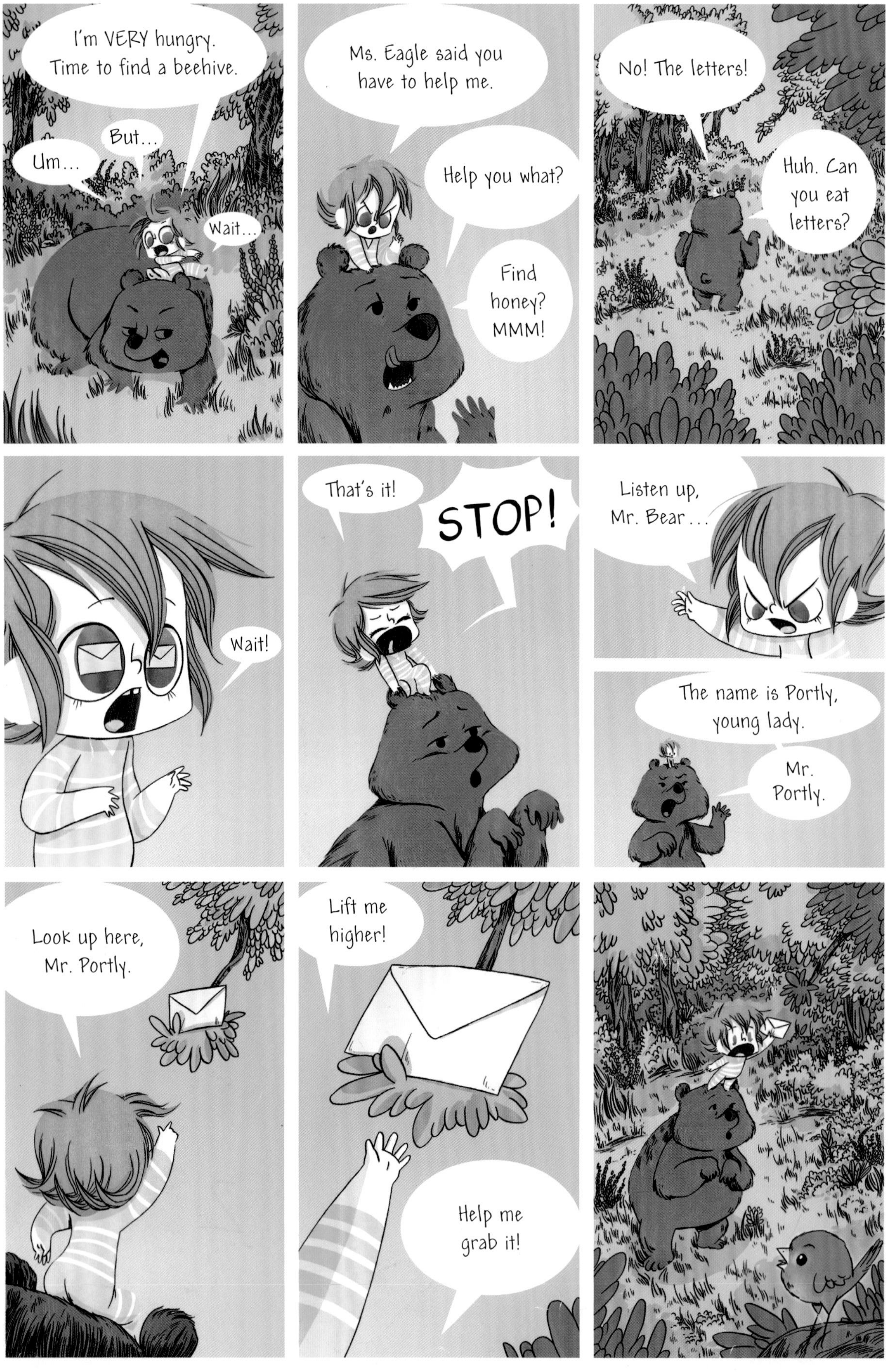

I'm VERY hungry. Time to find a beehive.
But...
Um...
Wait...
Ms. Eagle said you have to help me.
Help you what?
Find honey? MMM!
No! The letters!
Huh. Can you eat letters?
Wait!
That's it!
STOP!
Listen up, Mr. Bear...
The name is Portly, young lady.
Mr. Portly.
Look up here, Mr. Portly.
Lift me higher!
Help me grab it!

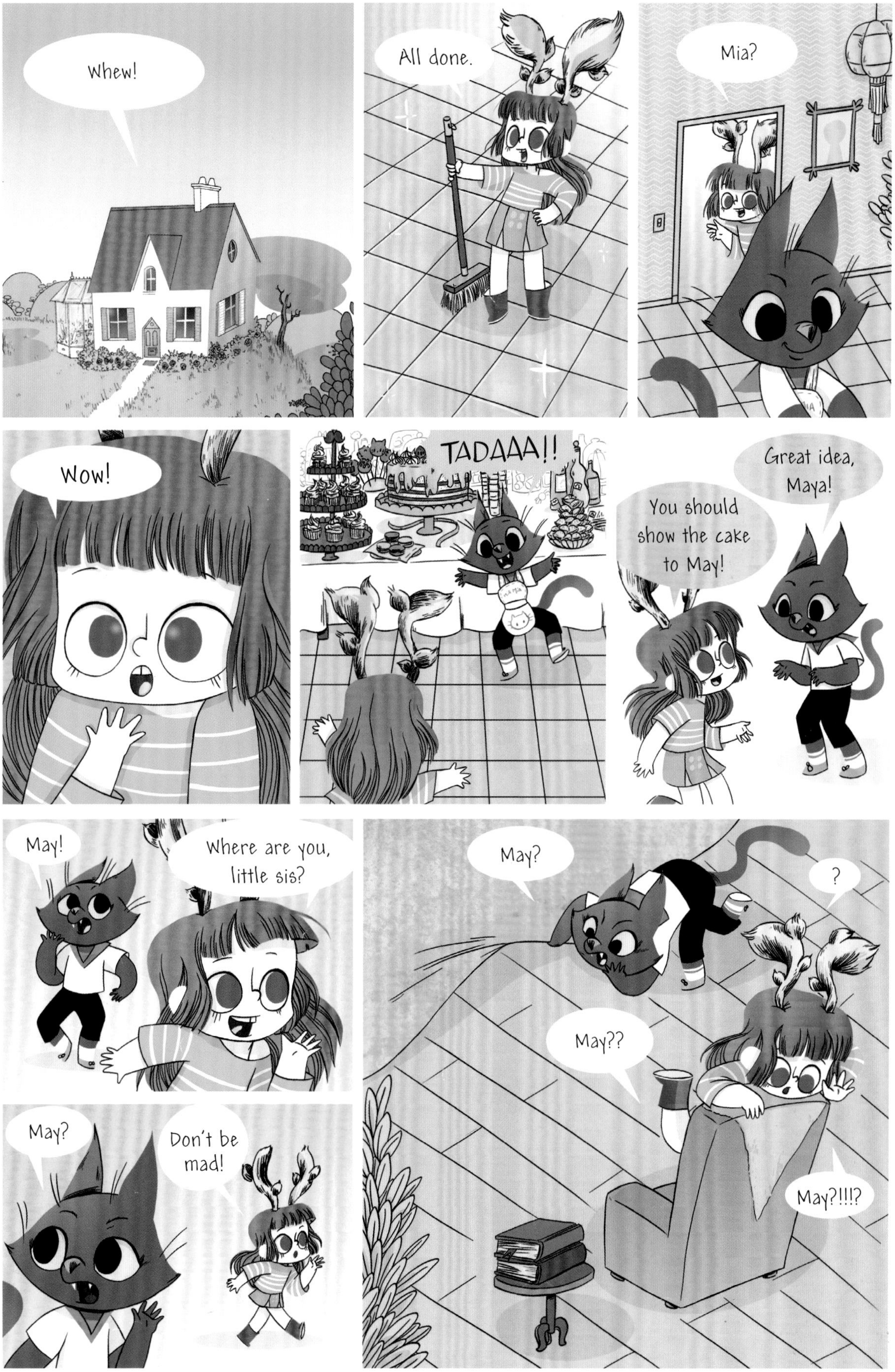
Whew!
All done.
Mia?
Wow!
TADAAA!!
Great idea, Maya!
You should show the cake to May!
May!
Where are you, little sis?
May?
?
May??
May?!!!?
May?
Don't be mad!

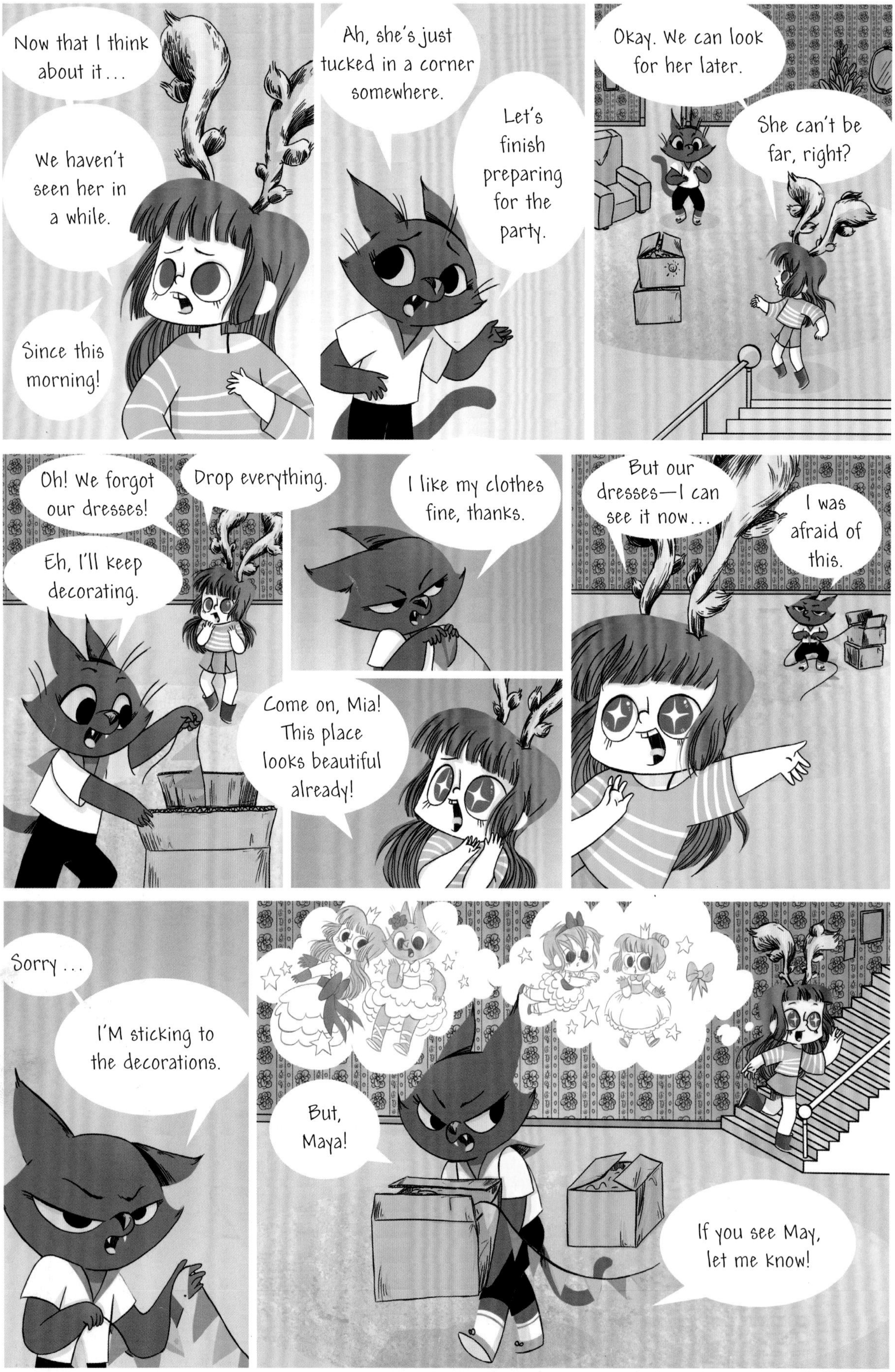

Now that I think about it...
We haven't seen her in a while.
Since this morning!
Ah, she's just tucked in a corner somewhere.
Let's finish preparing for the party.
Okay. We can look for her later.
She can't be far, right?
Oh! We forgot our dresses!
Drop everything.
Eh, I'll keep decorating.
I like my clothes fine, thanks.
Come on, Mia! This place looks beautiful already!
But our dresses—I can see it now...
I was afraid of this.
Sorry...
I'M sticking to the decorations.
But, Maya!
If you see May, let me know!

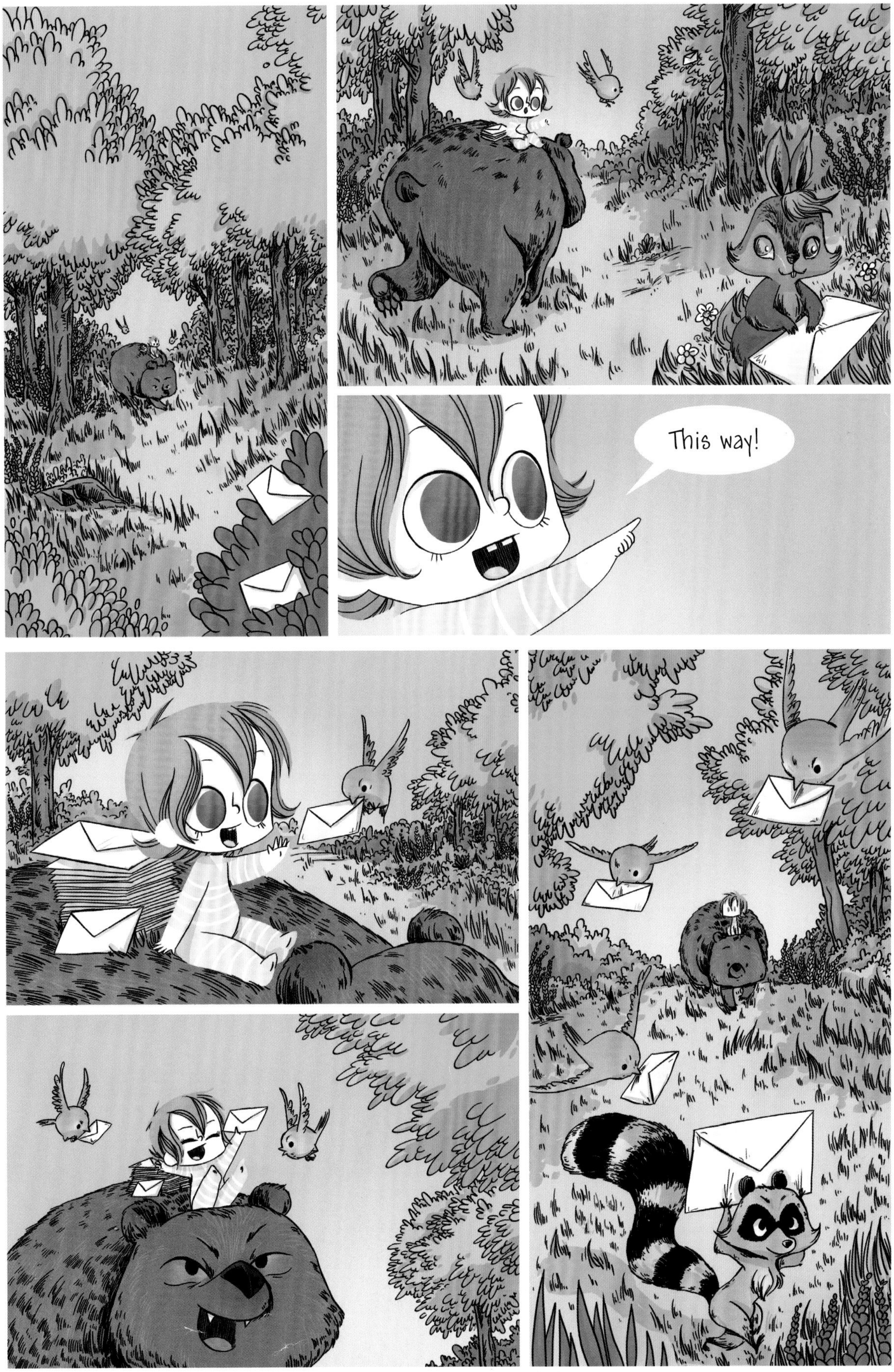
This way!

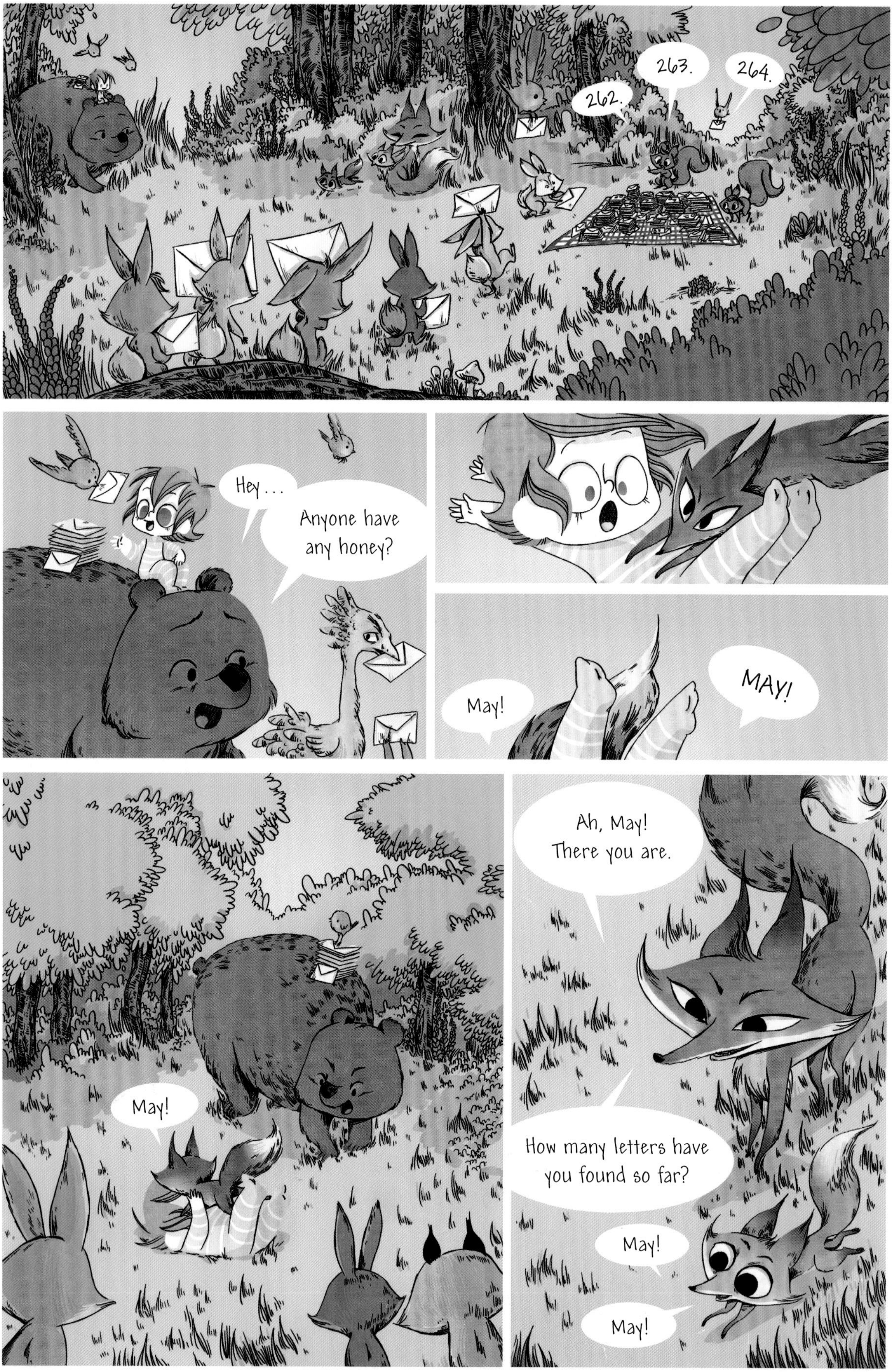
262.
263.
264.
Hey...
Anyone have any honey?
May!
MAY!
May!
Ah, May! There you are.
How many letters have you found so far?
May!
May!

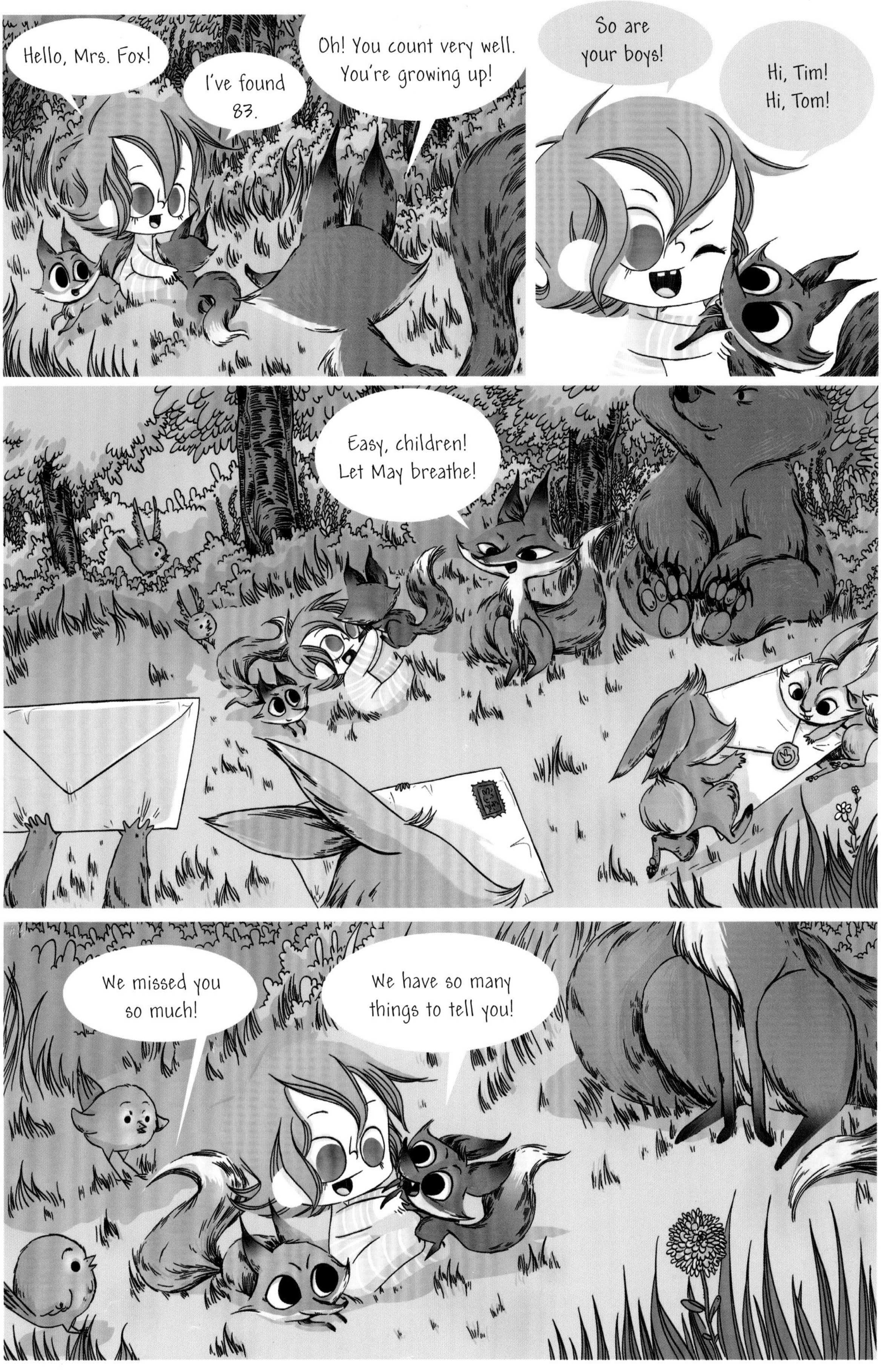
Hello, Mrs. Fox!
I've found 83.
Oh! You count very well. You're growing up!
So are your boys!
Hi, Tim! Hi, Tom!
Easy, children! Let May breathe!
We missed you so much!
We have so many things to tell you!

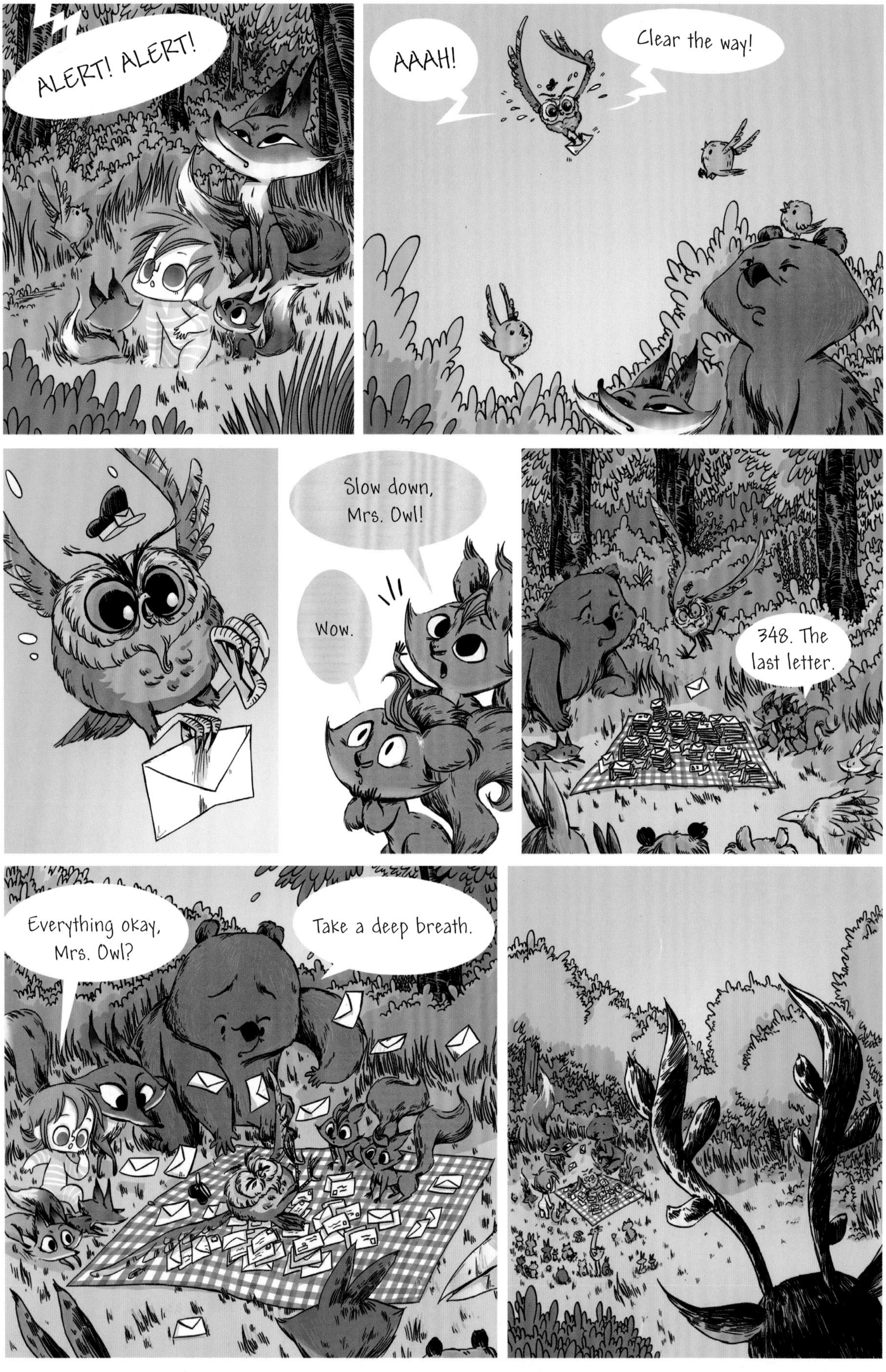
ALERT! ALERT!
AAAH!
Clear the way!
Slow down, Mrs. Owl!
Wow.
348. The last letter.
Everything okay, Mrs. Owl?
Take a deep breath.

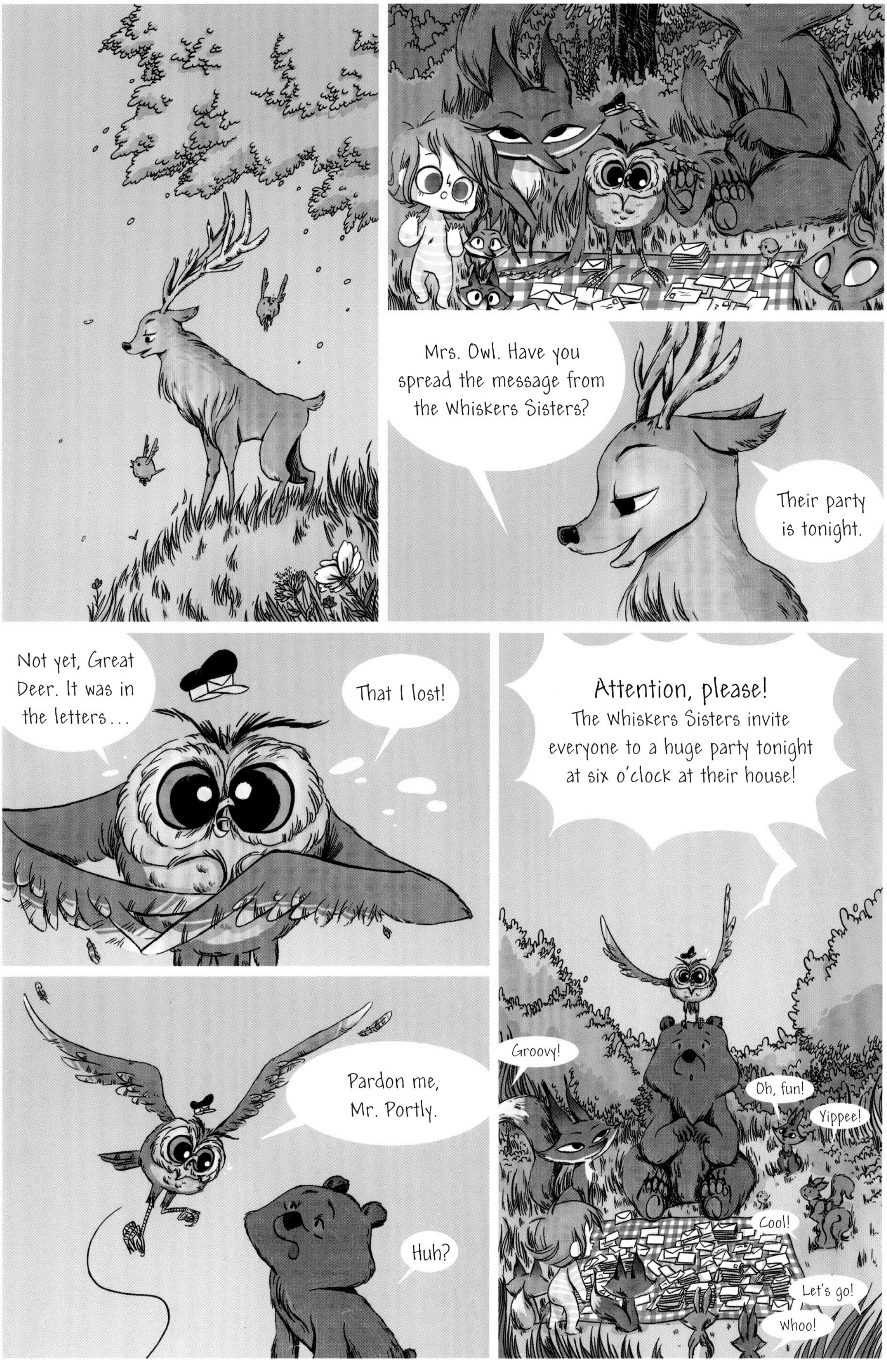
Mrs. Owl. Have you spread the message from the Whiskers Sisters?
Their party is tonight.
Not yet, Great Deer. It was in the letters...
That I lost!
Pardon me, Mr. Portly.
Huh?
Attention, please! The Whiskers Sisters invite everyone to a huge party tonight at six o'clock at their house!
Groovy!
Oh, fun!
Yippee!
Cool!
Let's go!
Whoo!

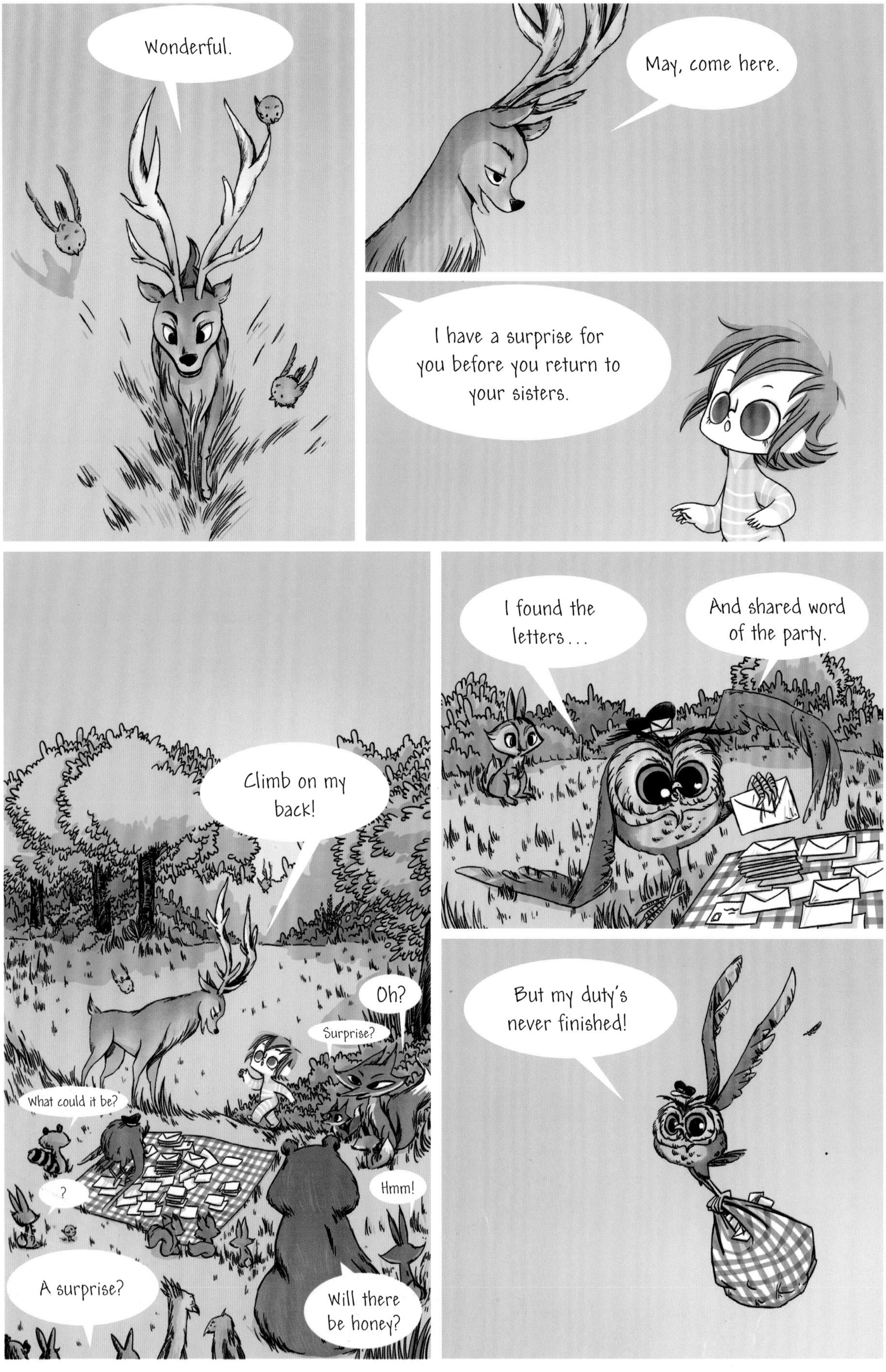
Wonderful.
May, come here.
I have a surprise for you before you return to your sisters.
Climb on my back!
Oh?
Surprise?
What could it be?
?
Hmm!
A surprise?
Will there be honey?
I found the letters...
And shared word of the party.
But my duty's never finished!

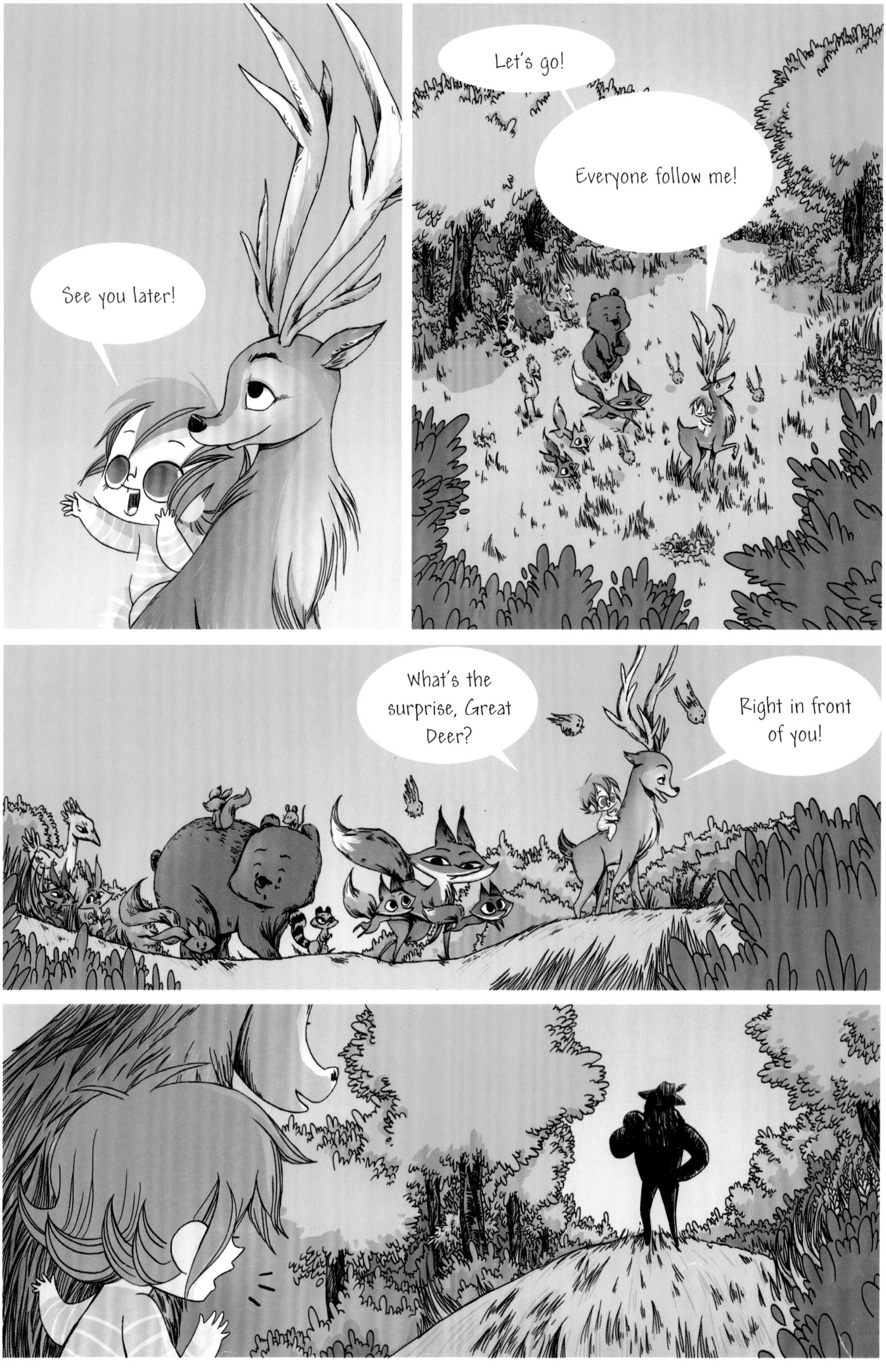
See you later!
Let's go!
Everyone follow me!
What's the surprise, Great Deer?
Right in front of you!

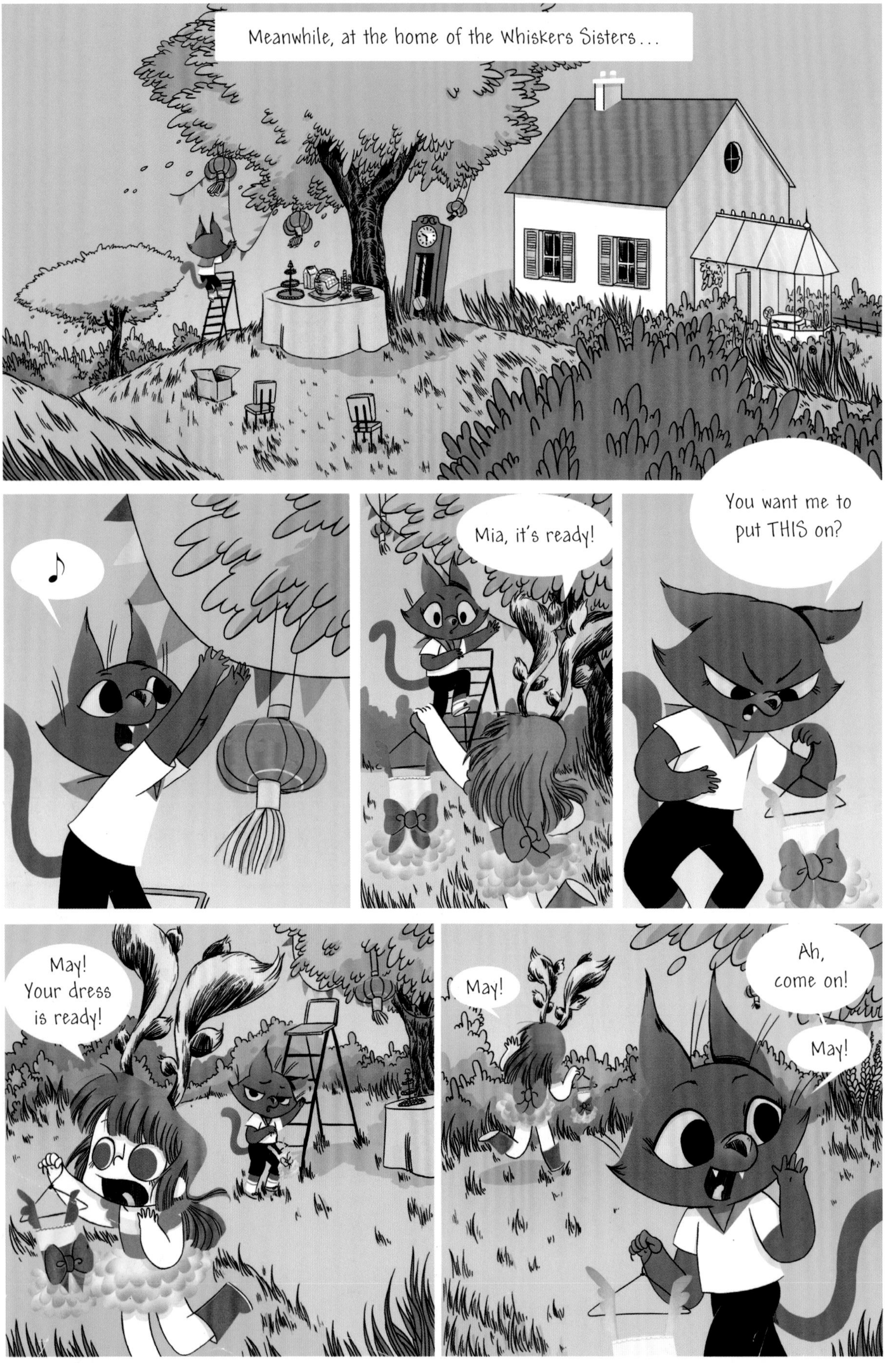
Meanwhile, at the home of the Whiskers Sisters...
♪
Mia, it's ready!
You want me to put THIS on?
May! Your dress is ready!
May!
Ah, come on!
May!

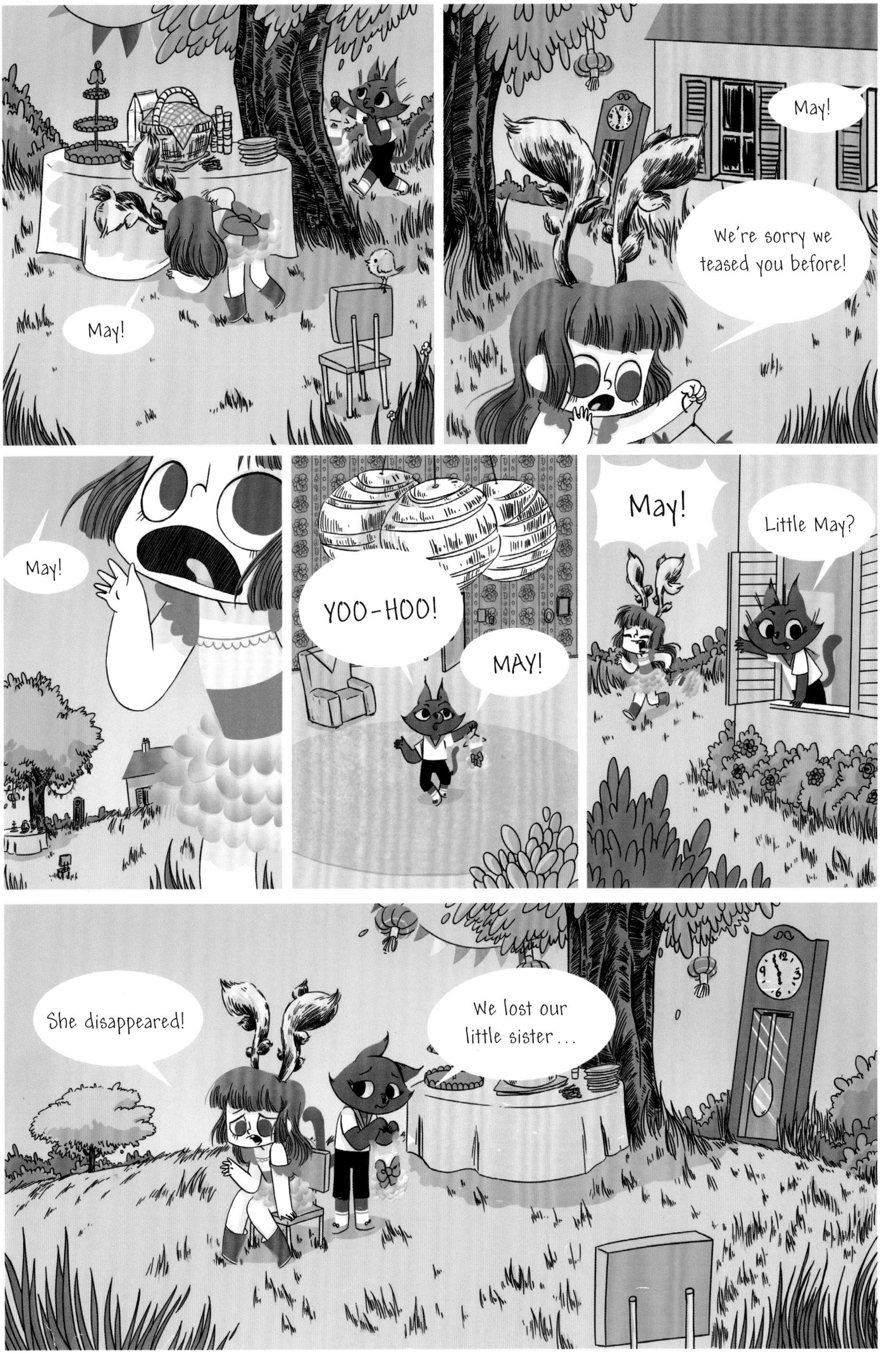
May!
May!
We're sorry we teased you before!
May!
YOO-HOO!
MAY!
May!
Little May?
She disappeared!
We lost our little sister...

We should've been nicer!

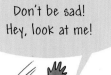

Don't be sad! Hey, look at me!

Our party is ruined!

Eh ... this dress doesn't fit so bad!

BOO-HOO

It will be okay!

"You never fail if you keep trying!"

DING   DING DONG

May is missing, and it's already six o'clock.

No one is here!

DONG DING DING DONG DING
DING DONG
DING DONG
DONG DING
DONG
DING

SIGH. You're right.

This party's a' bust.

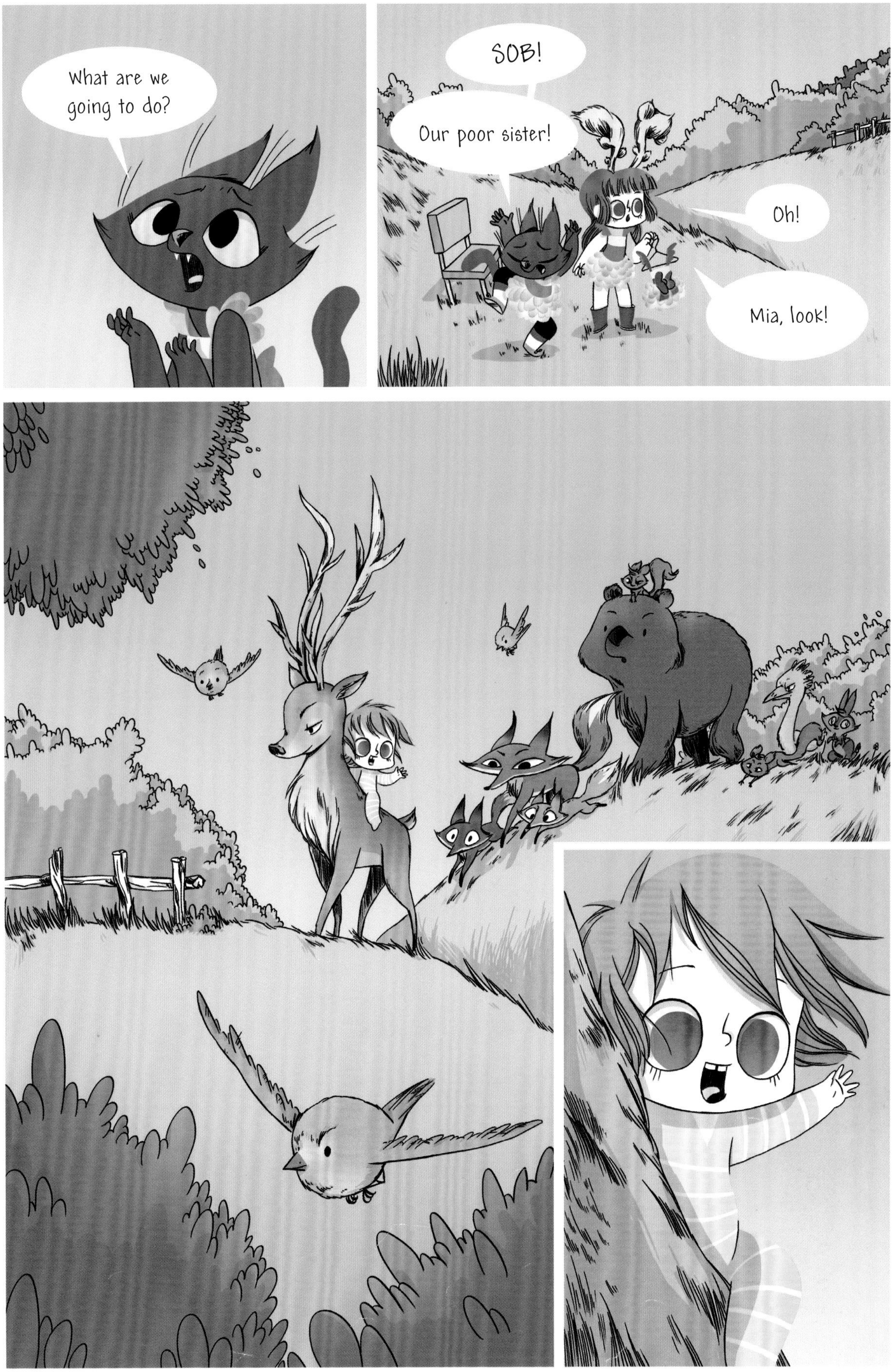
What are we going to do?
SOB!
Our poor sister!
Oh!
Mia, look!

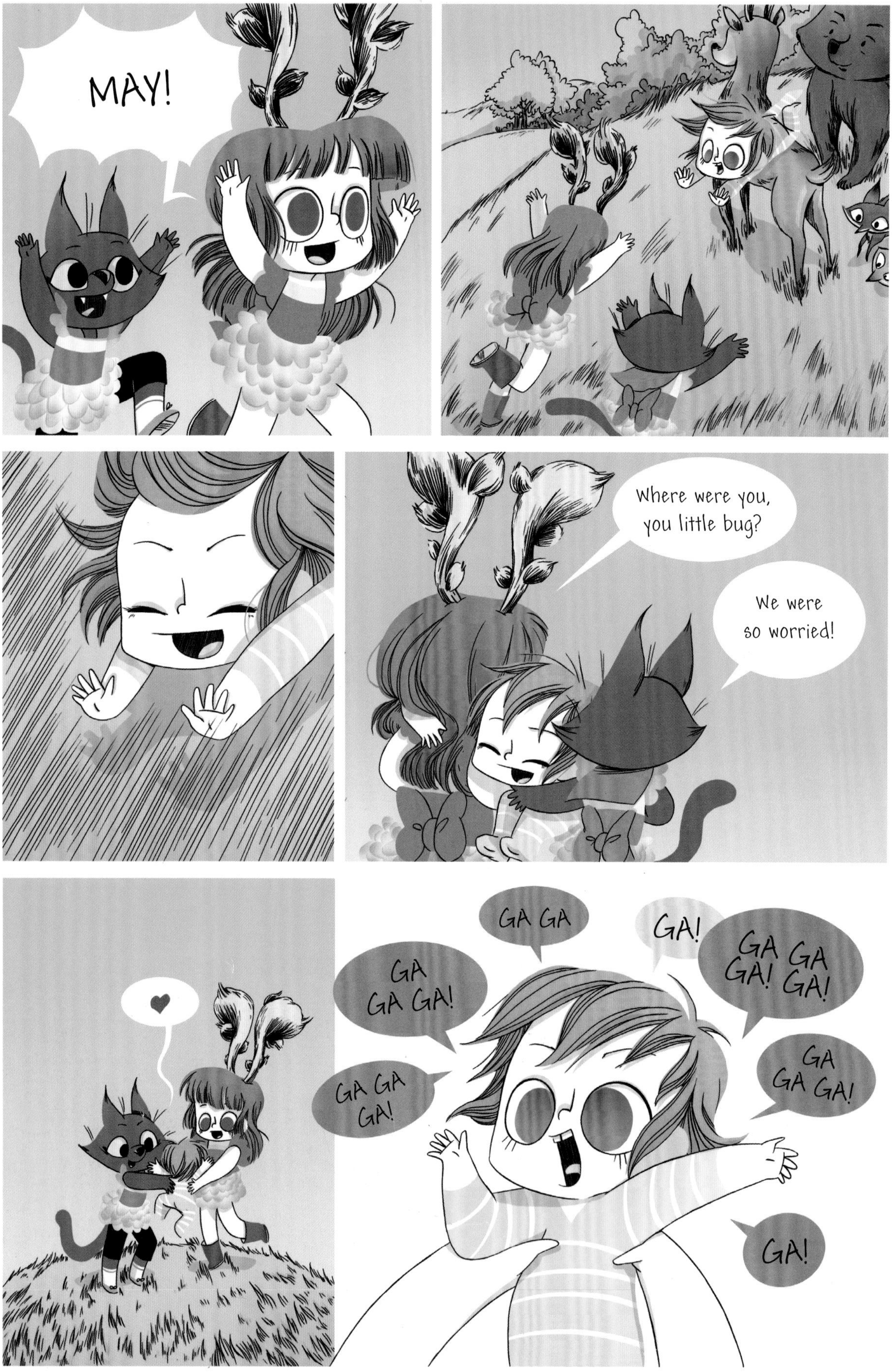
MAY!
Where were you, you little bug?
We were so worried!
GA GA
GA!
GA GA GA!
GA GA GA! GA!
GA GA GA!
GA GA GA!
GA GA GA!
GA!

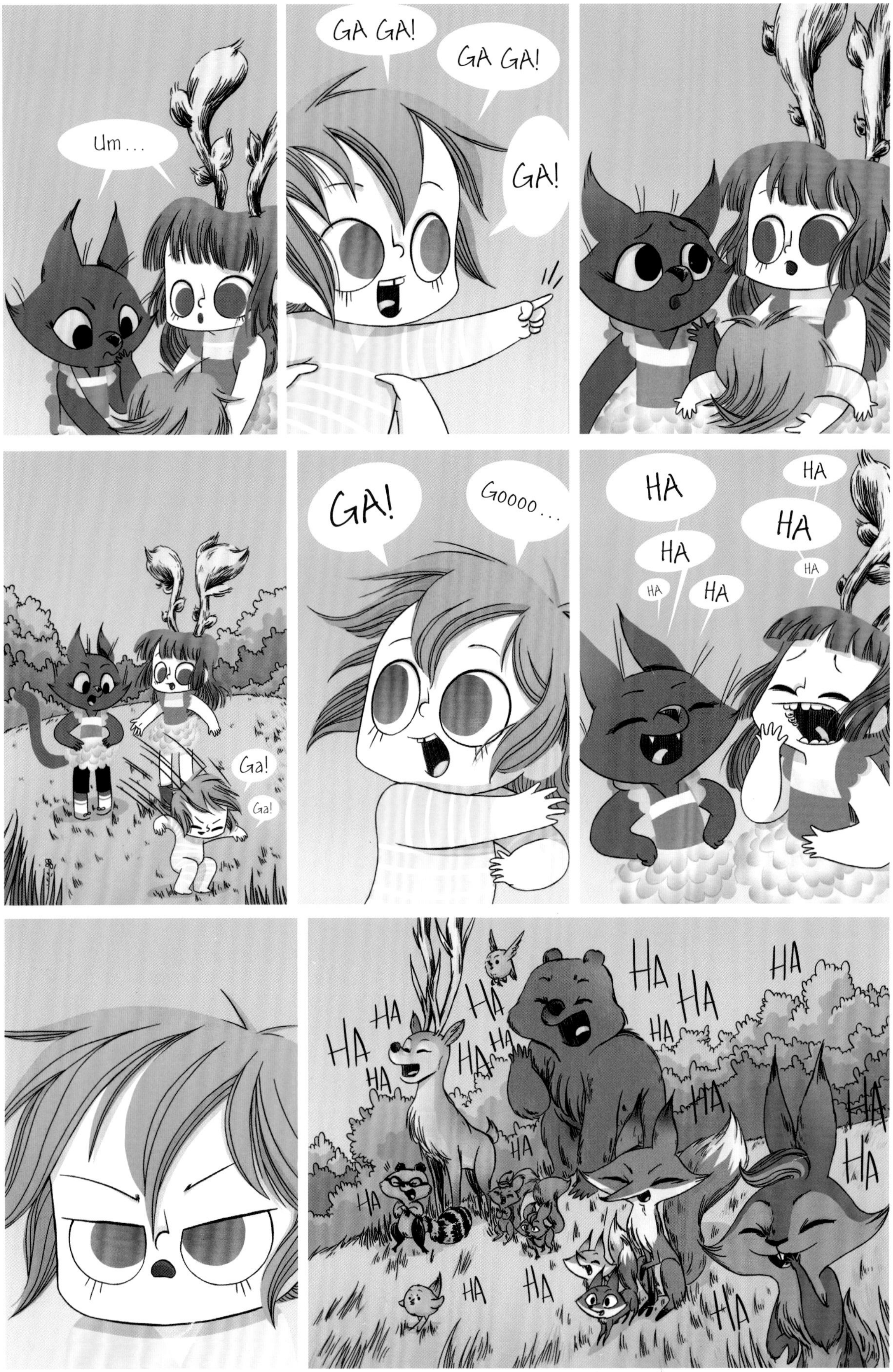
Um...
GA GA!
GA GA!
GA!
Ga!
Ga!
GA!
Goooo...
HA
HA
HA
HA
HA
HA
HA
HA HA HA HA HA HA HA HA HA HA HA HA HA HA HA HA HA HA

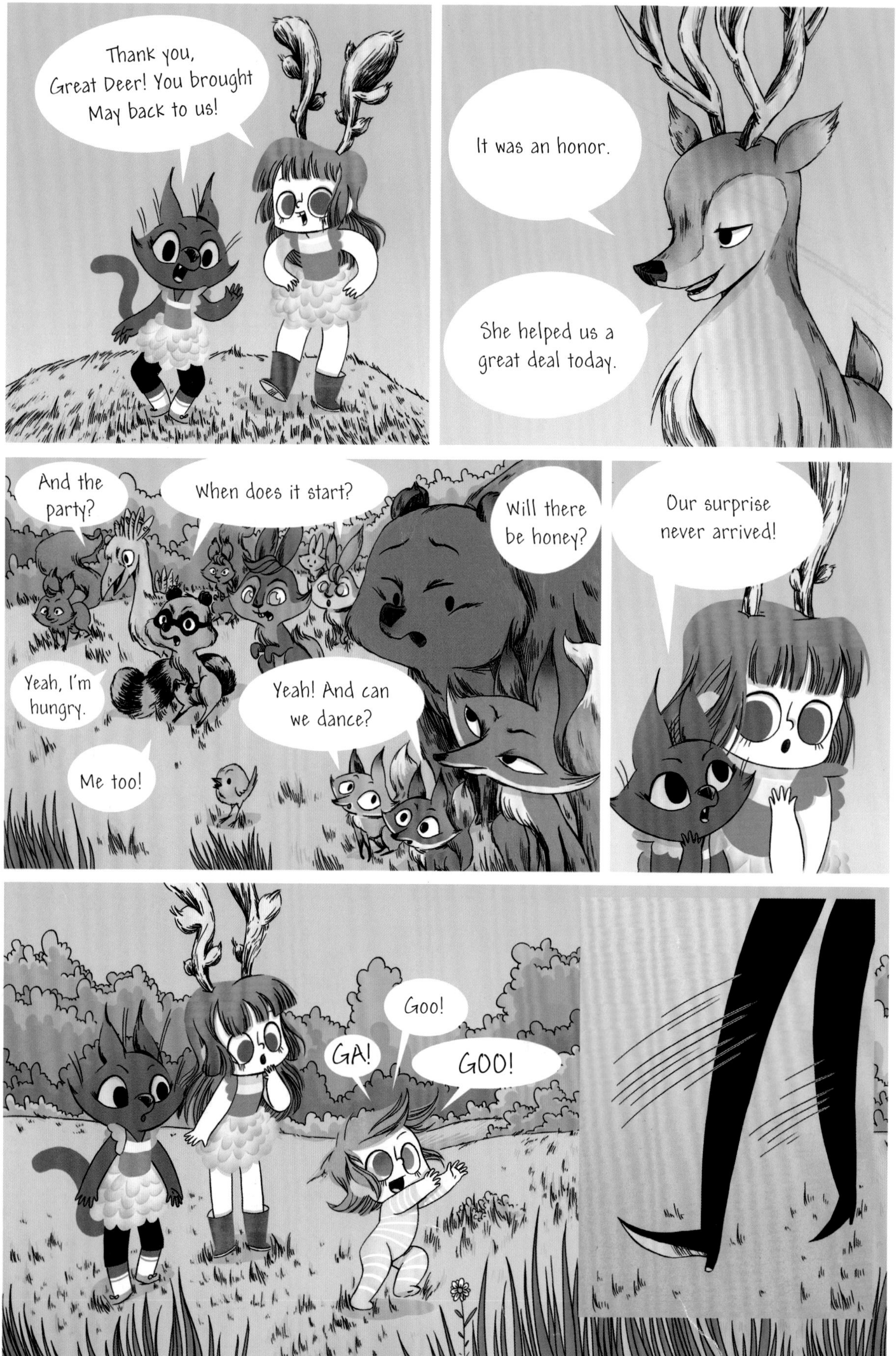
Thank you, Great Deer! You brought May back to us!
It was an honor.
She helped us a great deal today.
And the party?
When does it start?
Will there be honey?
Yeah, I'm hungry.
Yeah! And can we dance?
Me too!
Our surprise never arrived!
Goo!
GA!
GOO!

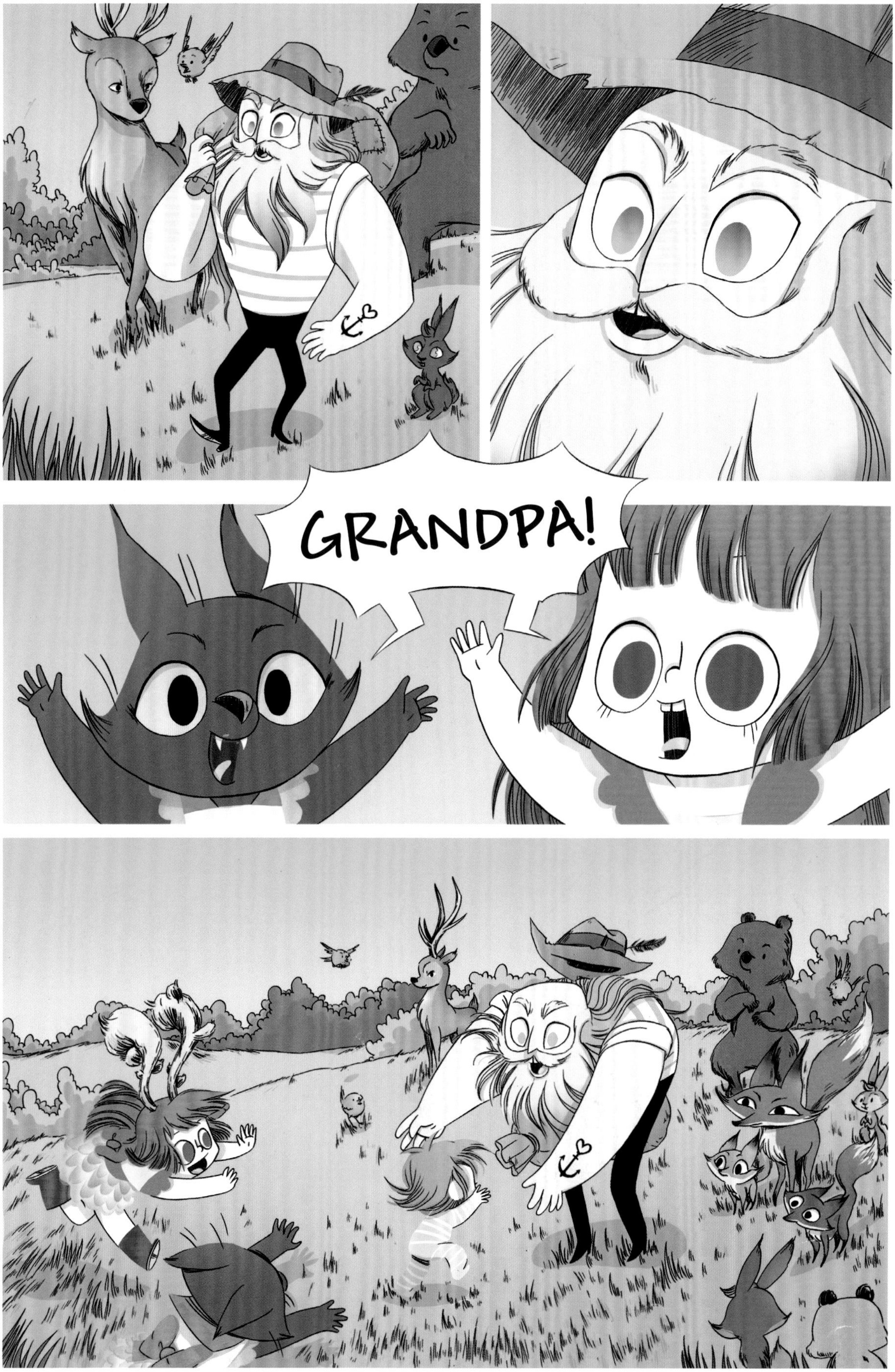
GRANDPA!

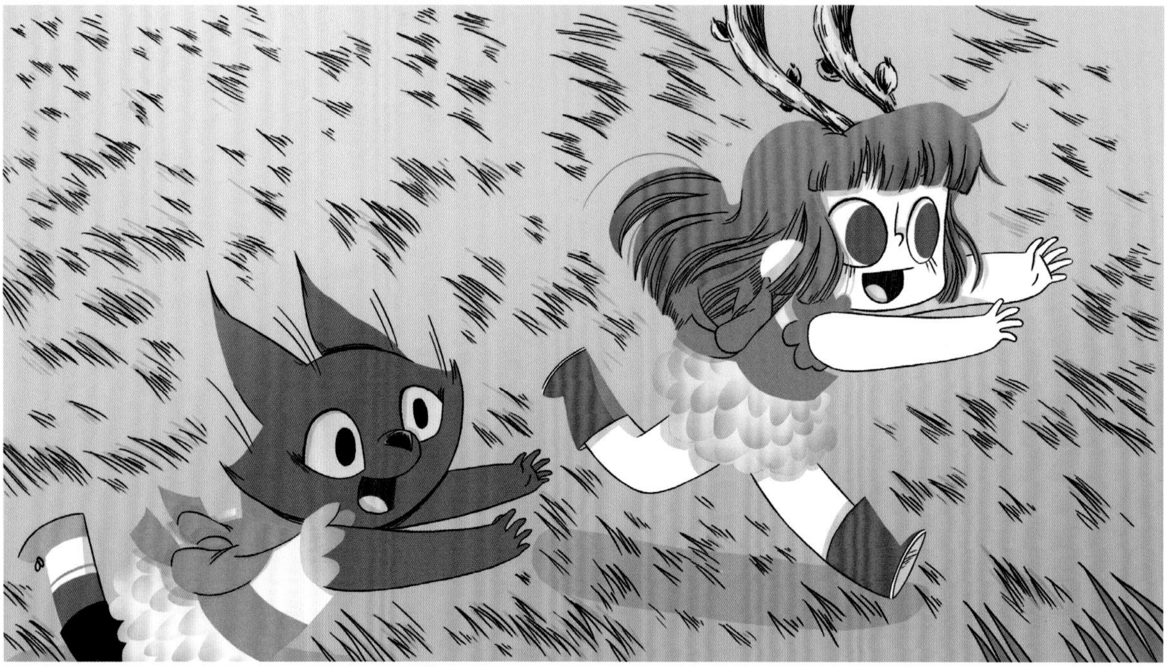

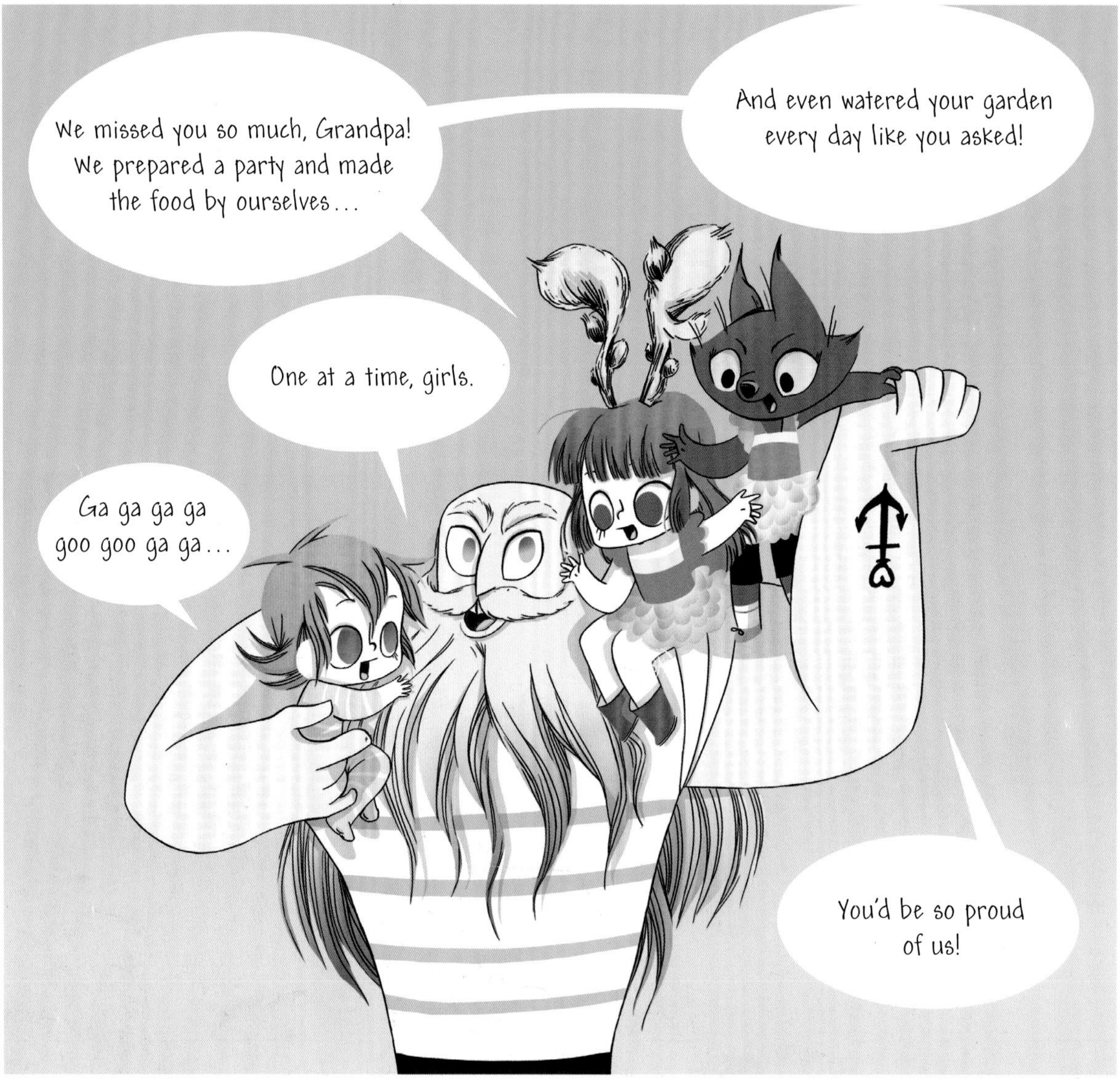
We missed you so much, Grandpa! We prepared a party and made the food by ourselves...
And even watered your garden every day like you asked!
One at a time, girls.
Ga ga ga ga goo goo ga ga...
You'd be so proud of us!

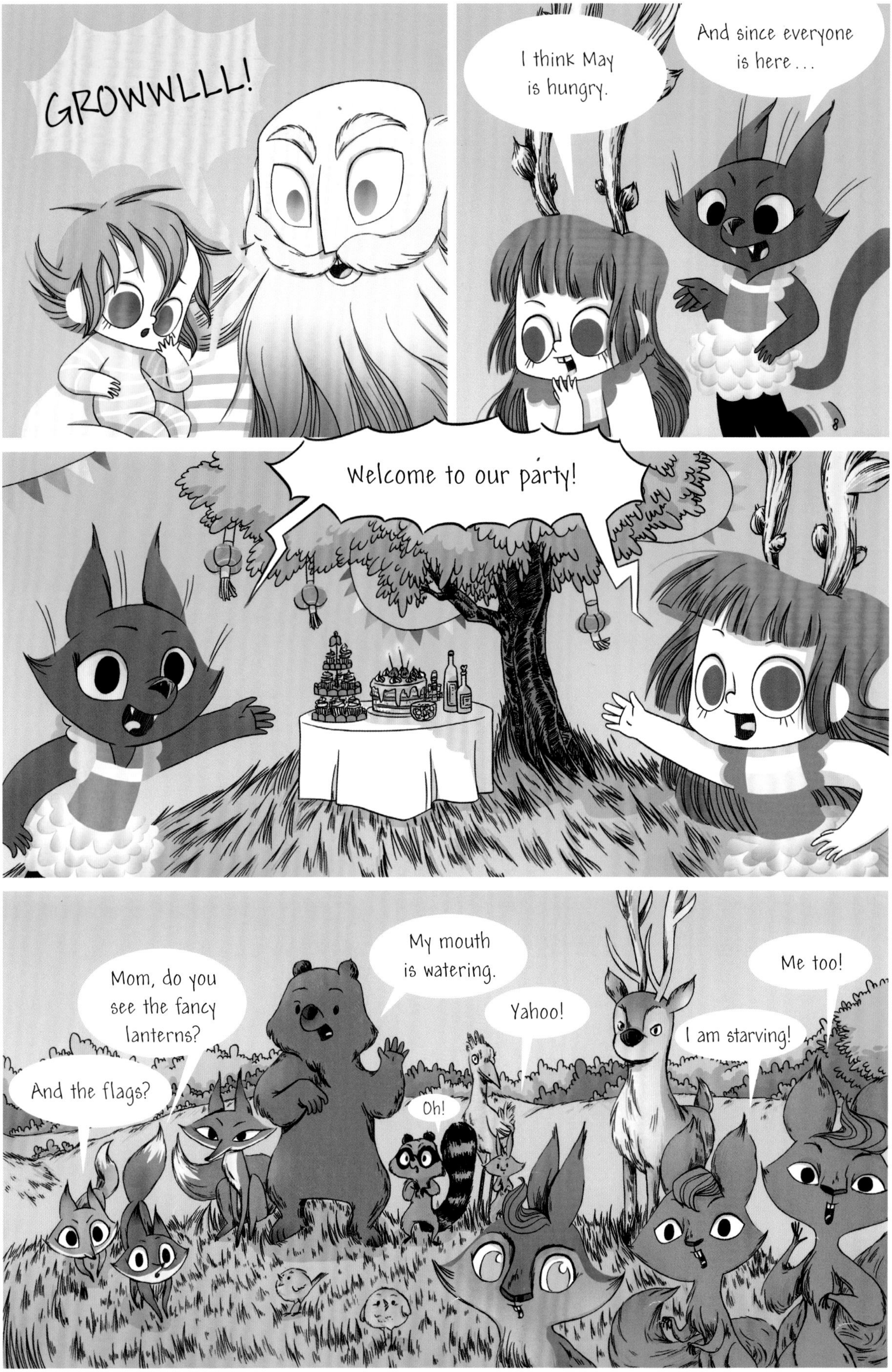
GROWWLLL!
I think May is hungry.
And since everyone is here . . .
Welcome to our party!
Mom, do you see the fancy lanterns?
And the flags?
My mouth is watering.
Oh!
Yahoo!
I am starving!
Me too!

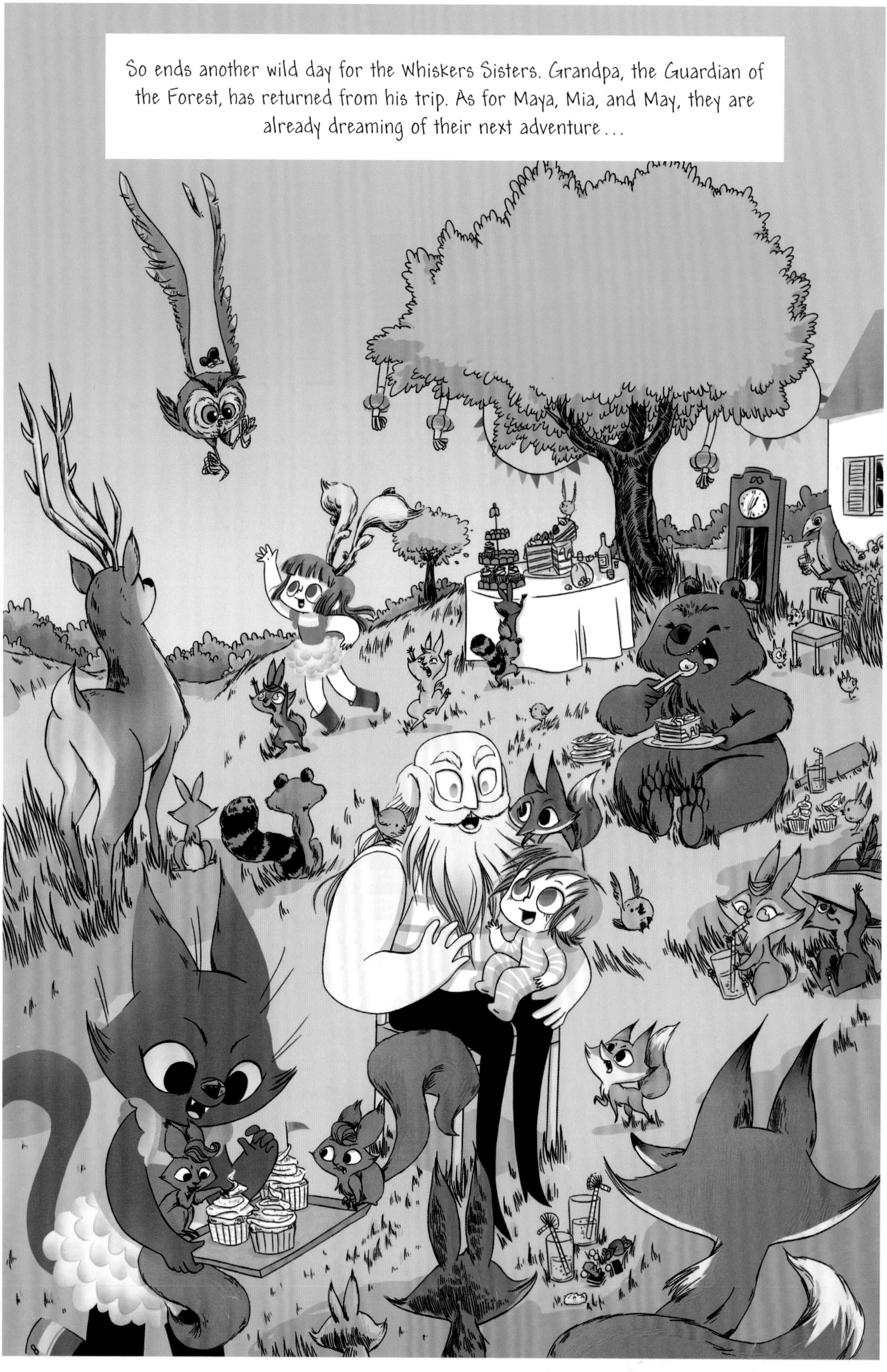
So ends another wild day for the Whiskers Sisters. Grandpa, the Guardian of the Forest, has returned from his trip. As for Maya, Mia, and May, they are already dreaming of their next adventure...

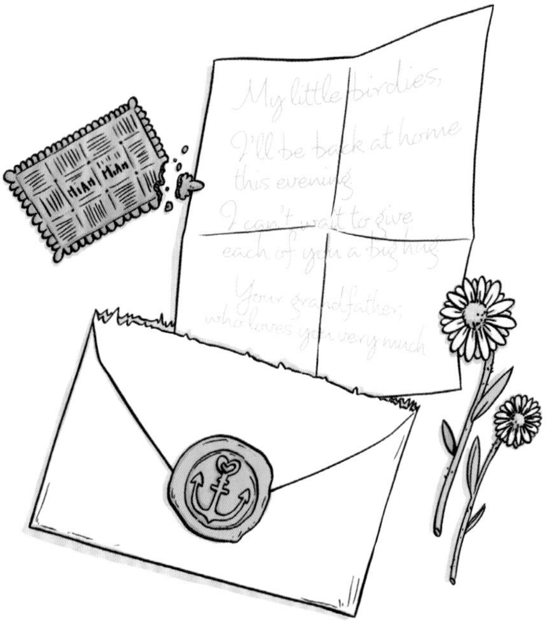
My little birdies,
I'll be back at home
this evening
I can't wait to give
each of you a big hug
Your grandfather,
who loves you very much
MIAM
MIAM

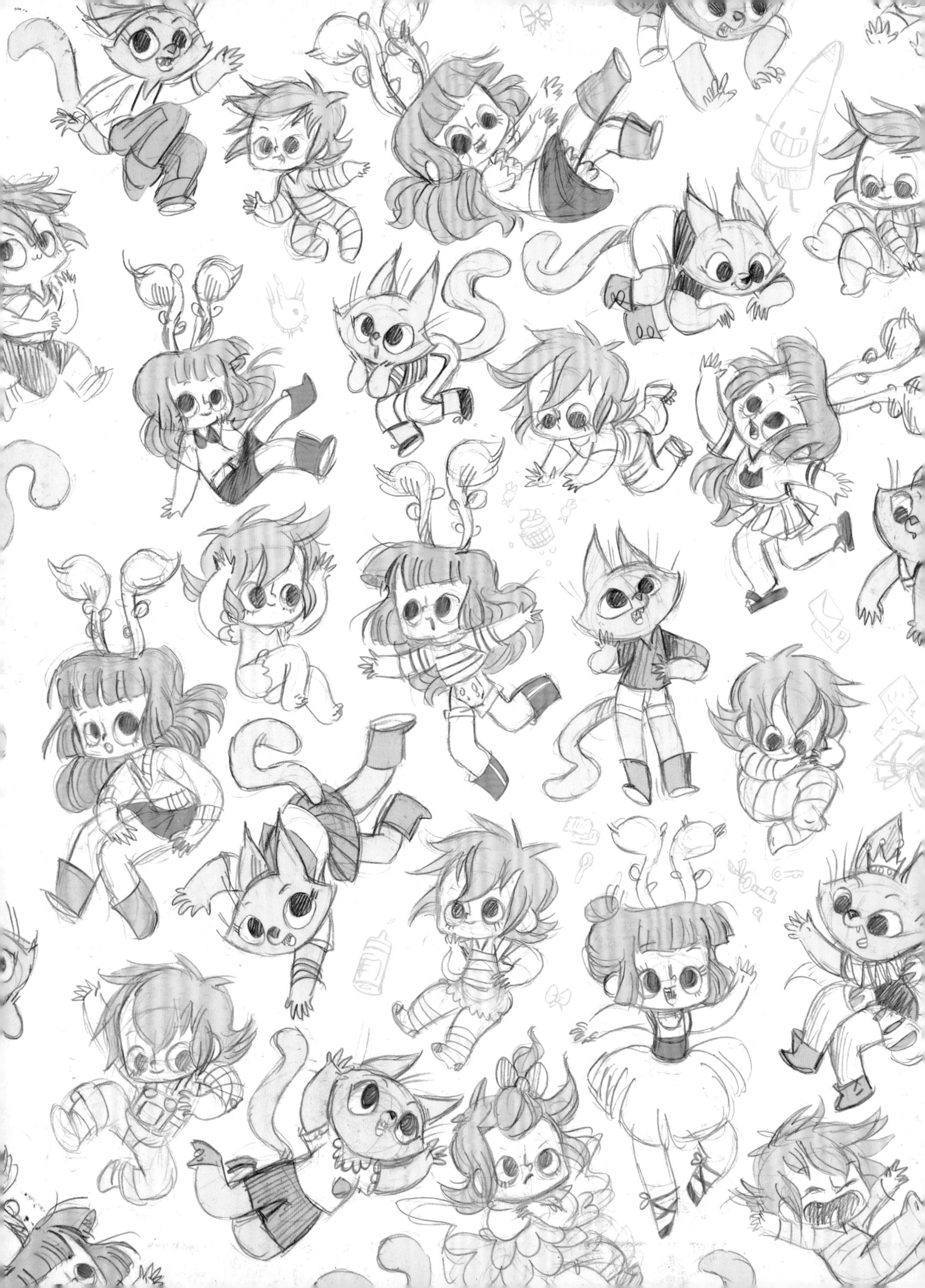